DEC

George's face was [illegible] with Robin. "Your au[illegible] our plans, Robin. You're staying right here. She can't send you three thousand miles away like you're her property."

A chill traveled up Robin's spine. George was doing the same thing her aunt was doing—deciding what was right for her without asking her what she thought! "Can you just take me home?" she asked.

"Sure. No problem."

The whole ride passed in dismal silence. She should have known better. George wasn't going to be impartial and objective about this. He wanted her to stay in California.

But as she stared out the window, George kept up an indignant running tirade. He accused everyone but himself of trying to run Robin's life for her. Finally he stopped speaking as he pulled the car up in front of the Wilsons' house.

"Don't—you don't have to come in, okay?"

George smiled. "I don't mind, Robin. You know I wouldn't leave you all alone."

But she shook her head vehemently, not trusting herself to meet his eyes. "No, that's not it. I really want to be alone for a while," she told him. Before he could protest, she jumped out of the car and hurried to the front door.

Bantam Books in the Sweet Valley High Series
Ask your bookseller for the books you have missed

#1 DOUBLE LOVE
#2 SECRETS
#3 PLAYING WITH FIRE
#4 POWER PLAY
#5 ALL NIGHT LONG
#6 DANGEROUS LOVE
#7 DEAR SISTER
#8 HEARTBREAKER
#9 RACING HEARTS
#10 WRONG KIND OF GIRL
#11 TOO GOOD TO BE TRUE
#12 WHEN LOVE DIES
#13 KIDNAPPED!
#14 DECEPTIONS
#15 PROMISES
#16 RAGS TO RICHES
#17 LOVE LETTERS
#18 HEAD OVER HEELS
#19 SHOWDOWN
#20 CRASH LANDING!
#21 RUNAWAY
#22 TOO MUCH IN LOVE
#23 SAY GOODBYE
#24 MEMORIES
#25 NOWHERE TO RUN
#26 HOSTAGE!
#27 LOVESTRUCK
#28 ALONE IN THE CROWD
#29 BITTER RIVALS
#30 JEALOUS LIES
#31 TAKING SIDES
#32 THE NEW JESSICA
#33 STARTING OVER
#34 FORBIDDEN LOVE
#35 OUT OF CONTROL
#36 LAST CHANCE
#37 RUMORS
#38 LEAVING HOME
#39 SECRET ADMIRER
#40 ON THE EDGE
#41 OUTCAST
#42 CAUGHT IN THE MIDDLE
#43 HARD CHOICES
#44 PRETENSES
#45 FAMILY SECRETS
#46 DECISIONS

Super Editions: PERFECT SUMMER
SPECIAL CHRISTMAS
SPRING BREAK
MALIBU SUMMER
WINTER CARNIVAL
SPRING FEVER

Super Thrillers: DOUBLE JEOPARDY
ON THE RUN

SWEET VALLEY HIGH

DECISIONS

Written by
Kate William

Created by
FRANCINE PASCAL

BANTAM BOOKS
TORONTO • NEW YORK • LONDON • SYDNEY • AUCKLAND

RL 6, IL age 12 and up

DECISIONS

A Bantam Book / July 1988

Conceived by Francine Pascal.

Produced by Daniel Weiss Associates, Inc.
27 West 20th Street
New York, NY 10011

Cover art by James Mathewuse

ISBN 0-553-27278-0

Published simultaneously in the United States and Canada

Bantam Books are published by Bantam Books, a division of Bantam Doubleday Dell Publishing Group, Inc. Its trademark, consisting of the words "Bantam Books" and the portrayal of a rooster, is Registered in U.S. Patent and Trademark Office and in other countries. Marca Registrada. Bantam Books, 666 Fifth Avenue, New York, New York 10103.

PRINTED IN THE UNITED STATES OF AMERICA

O 0 9 8 7 6 5 4 3 2 1

DECISIONS

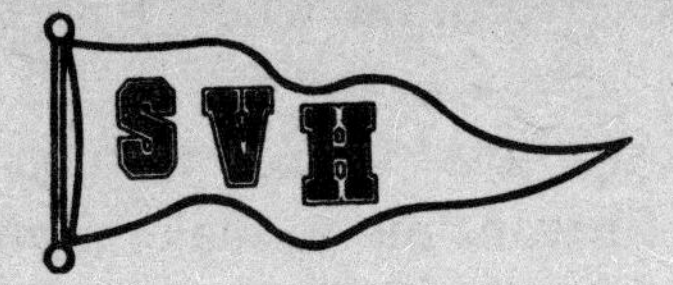

One

With a flick of her wrist, Elizabeth Wakefield snapped open *The Oracle* to the second page. She ran her eyes down her weekly gossip column, "Eyes and Ears." Oblivious of the students who were passing by on their way to have lunch, Elizabeth smiled to herself. Even after months of writing for the school newspaper, she still got a rush every time she saw her words in black and white.

One day, she told herself, *I'll see my name on the cover of a book!*

Still grinning, she tucked the paper under one arm and turned to twirl the dial of her combination lock.

"Liz, where have you *been*? I've been looking for you for *ages*!" Jessica, Elizabeth's identical twin sister, came bouncing up to Elizabeth. "You're never around when I need to talk to you!"

"What's up, Jess? Critical fashion news from Lila? Or you want me to make dinner? Or you need a favor? Which is it?" A dimple appeared in her left cheek as Elizabeth teased her twin.

Jessica pouted. "How can you say that? I don't ask you to do *that* many favors for me, do I?"

"I'm not going to answer that," Elizabeth replied.

"It's only because you're the sweetest, nicest, best sister in the world," Jessica continued, leaning against the set of lockers. "I just naturally turn to my big sister for guidance."

Holding back a giggle, Elizabeth gave her twin a light punch on the shoulder. All kidding aside, Jessica did turn to her very often, and had for most of their sixteen years. But Elizabeth turned to Jessica, too. It was simply a part of being identical twins, as Elizabeth had figured out a long time ago. It was impossible to imagine going through an entire day without relying on each other in some way.

And Elizabeth knew it was her responsibility to keep Jessica firmly on the ground. Otherwise, Elizabeth thought, her twin might fly off into the ozone layer. Jessica's style was fast, impetuous, and adventure-seeking. She only stayed in one place long enough to capture another boy's heart or lead the cheerleading squad through practice.

But where Jessica was a whirlwind, Elizabeth was thoughtful, introspective, and studious. Of course, she loved spending time at the beach and going to parties, too. But she spent those times talking and laughing with her closest friends instead of flitting around in a breathless social whirl the way her twin did.

Those were the inner differences, though, and it took most people awhile to understand that identical twins were only identical on the surface. On the outside, it was nearly impossible to tell the two apart. Both of them could pose as models for the California girl, with perfect size-six figures and sun-kissed shoulder-length hair, their golden tans set off by sparkling eyes the color of the Pacific. They each had a dimple that showed up whenever they smiled, and they each wore identical gold lavaliere necklaces, presents from their parents on the twins' sixteenth birthday.

"So what's so life-and-death that you have to tell me?" Elizabeth asked as she pushed her locker shut.

"I just wanted to *remind* you that I'm starting my new baby-sitting job after school, so you'll have to get a ride home from Jeffrey," said Jessica.

As usual, Jessica was suffering from a shortage of spending money. She had asked their older brother, Steven, to keep an eye on the bulletin board at the state university and to let her know of any jobs that were available. Over the weekend he had given her a phone number, and she had arranged to baby-sit a few days a week for the little sister of a music student, Alex Kane. Alex was very busy with an important composition project for his senior thesis, and because his parents worked all day, he wanted someone to keep his little sister from disturbing him while he composed.

"I didn't forget," Elizabeth said. "And I already asked him."

Tall, handsome Jeffrey French was Elizabeth's steady boyfriend. Fortunately he was generous about giving her rides whenever she needed them, because Jessica had a way of appropriating the red Fiat convertible the twins shared. Jessica always seemed to find a convincing reason why she absolutely had to have the car.

"I hope this job turns out OK," Jessica muttered as they turned toward the cafeteria. "I don't know—do you think he might turn out to be one of those eccentric musicians?"

Elizabeth shrugged and then smiled at some

friends as they walked down the hall. "Not necessarily, Jess. If he's living at home while he works on this big composition and he needs to concentrate, I can see how he'd want someone to watch his little sister."

"I guess," Jessica said skeptically.

"Well, just don't worry about it. Besides," Elizabeth added, "you need the money, right?"

Rolling her eyes, Jessica sighed. Her good friend, Lila Fowler, was one of the richest girls in Sweet Valley, and Jessica was constantly broke just trying to keep her wardrobe and her record collection up with Lila's. And then there were all the other indispensable necessities of life, as she was always telling Elizabeth, such as tanning lotion, makeup, concert tickets, milk shakes at the Dairi Burger . . .

"Right," Jessica said. "I need the money. There's a new bathing suit at Lisette's, and I've got to have it or I'll just shrivel up and die."

Elizabeth giggled and pushed open the cafeteria door. "I don't think that's likely, Jess."

For a moment the twins stood at the entrance to the cafeteria, each of them silently scanning the crowd for her particular friends. The cafeteria hummed with a dull roar of talking and laughter, chairs scraping across the floor, soda cans dropping down from the soda machine, and cash registers rattling.

"Where is Lila?" Jessica scowled across the room. "Hey," she went on, touching her sister's arm, "there's Robin. That reminds me, did I tell you what she said yesterday when I went over to her house to talk about cheerleading?"

Elizabeth raised her eyebrows. "Noo," she drawled. Reporting what people said was one of Jessica's favorite activities.

"She said she applied early admission to Sarah Lawrence College—you know, in New York? *And* she was accepted," Jessica announced with a significant look.

Surprised, Elizabeth glanced across the room to where Robin Wilson, Jessica's co-captain on the cheerleading squad, was sitting with Annie Whitman. One of the brightest girls in their junior class, Robin juggled excellent grades with cheerleading and participating in the community diving program. She had confided in Elizabeth many times about her hopes and aspirations, and Elizabeth knew Robin was determined to get the best possible education.

"You're kidding!" Elizabeth exclaimed. "She never said anything to me about it. You have to have perfect grades to be able to skip senior year and go straight to college."

"That's not all," Jessica continued in a hushed tone, her eyes wide with meaning. "As soon as she told me, she practically burst into hysterics."

"What?"

"Crying."

Elizabeth frowned, puzzled. "Hmm . . . that's strange. But, still, I'm impressed that she got accepted. I bet she'll do well."

With a shrug Jessica replied, "If she goes."

"Well, of course she will—why else would she have applied?" Elizabeth said with an incredulous laugh.

Jessica shrugged again. "Who knows? Hey, there's Lila. I'll see you later."

"Robin? I said what did you get on your chem quiz?"

Flushing, Robin Wilson put down her can of diet soda and met Annie Whitman's bright green eyes. "Oh, A minus. Sorry, Annie, I guess I'm a little distracted."

Annie looked at Robin with a sympathetic expression. "Still trying to decide about school?"

"Yeah." Propping her chin up on her hands, Robin sighed. "But I'm really not sure what to do! I mean, if I go to Sarah Lawrence, Aunt Fiona will pay for it all—and that's a lot of money."

Annie frowned. "But I don't see why she can't just pay for whatever college you want to go to. Why does it have to be Sarah Lawrence?"

"Family tradition, that's why," Robin replied

in a dry tone. "*She* went there, and my grandmother went there, so *I* have to go there. She'll pay if I go there, but not somewhere else."

Letting out a deep sigh, Robin swept her wavy brown hair off her forehead and frowned down at her lunch. Her aunt was a brilliant, successful artist, and when their parents died, she had raised Robin's mother almost single-handedly. Money and success after years of struggling had made her used to getting her own way.

And ever since Robin could remember, her aunt had been extremely generous to the Wilsons—but only when she wanted to be, and only if they played their part by being very grateful for the help they needed. She was opinionated, domineering, and impatient, but that was because she had had to fight so hard to get where she was. But as much as Robin admired her aunt's success, and appreciated the help, it was hard to *like* her. And that made it hard for Robin to swallow the idea of her aunt paying her entire college bill.

Forcing her thoughts back to the present, Robin shook her head again. "There's just so much to decide, that's the problem. But if I don't go there, I can't go anywhere. My mother can't afford to send me to school herself."

"Why not a state university?" Annie suggested.

"Yeah, I know. And UCLA has a good computer science program, too. But it still isn't free."

"What does George think?"

At the mention of George Warren's name, Robin blushed and dropped her eyes. She and Annie had become close friends from being on the cheerleading squad together, but there were certain things Robin couldn't tell Annie. One of them was that she hadn't even mentioned to her boyfriend that she had applied to college in the East.

"Oh, you know," she stalled. Finally she looked up at her friend. "Actually, he doesn't know about it."

"What?" Annie gasped, setting her soda can down with a thump. "How could you not tell him something so important?"

"I just—I knew he'd be upset, that's why. He thinks I'll be staying here in California and that I would never even want to go somewhere else."

"Well, *do* you want to go to Sarah Lawrence?"

Robin winced. "I don't know! I don't know what I want," she continued moodily. "I can't even think. I'm supposed to be getting myself ready mentally for the diving competition, and I can't even concentrate on that, or schoolwork, or cheerleading, let alone make one of the most important decisions of my *life*!"

Annie raised her eyebrows in surprise. "Robin,"

she said gently, "take it easy. You're going to drive yourself into the loony bin."

"I know, I know." Slumping back in her chair, Robin allowed herself a self-mocking smile as she looked at her friend. "Either that or I'll start stuffing myself with every fattening thing in sight!"

"No, no! Not that!" Annie laughed.

For years Robin had been overweight. Eating had been the biggest part of her life, and it didn't seem like a problem until she ran into Jessica Wakefield and the Pi Beta Alpha sorority. Because she wanted to be a member, Robin had done whatever pledge tasks the sorority sisters asked her to. And in the end Robin had still been blackballed—because she was fat.

After that, Robin started exercising and dieting seriously—not to impress the girls in the sorority, but to prove to herself she could do it. Shedding the pounds had transformed Robin, and she found she was a very attractive, even beautiful girl. Since then, she had become co-captain of the cheerleading squad and a very good platform diver, using athletic talents she had never known she had. But whenever she was upset or depressed, she had to fight the urge to binge on ice-cream sundaes or pizza.

"Don't worry," Robin said. "Every time I go to diving practice and see myself in a bathing suit, I say 'Don't eat—don't eat.' So far it's worked."

Annie smiled. "Don't get so worked up about this college stuff, OK? I know it's important, but it shouldn't drive you crazy."

Robin managed a grin. "OK, OK!"

"And don't you think you should tell George?" Annie continued tentatively. "I mean, won't he be kind of upset when he finds out you waited this long already?"

Robin slumped even further in her seat. *Upset* wasn't the word. She and George were supposed to be in love, not keeping secrets from each other. When they fell in love, he was still dating Enid Rollins, and secrecy had been a big part of their lives. But since that time, they had promised not to lie or hide the truth from anyone, especially each other. She sighed and pushed the straw into her soda can. "Yes. I know I have to tell him. But I'm really not looking forward to it."

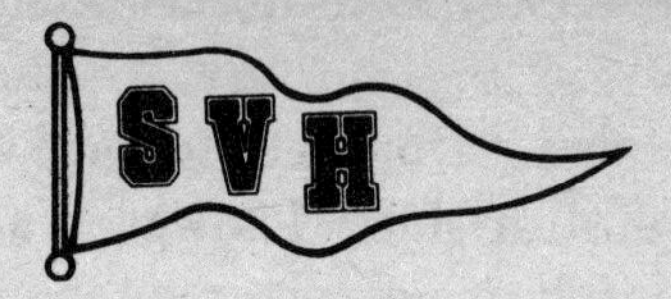

Two

A salt-scented breeze blew through Jessica's hair as she turned the Fiat onto the coast highway. A smile of pure satisfaction spread across her face. If there was one thing Jessica loved, it was driving with the top down!

And if she could only be sure that this job was going to turn out all right, she'd be perfectly happy. Alexander Kane had *sounded* nice enough and normal enough on the phone. However, Jessica's past adventures in baby-sitting had sometimes turned out to have horrible surprises. But she was ready to keep an open mind. Besides, as Elizabeth had reminded her, she needed the money.

She was humming to the song on the radio when she spotted the cedar-shingled bungalow with white shutters she was looking for.

"Seventeen twenty-nine," she murmured, stopping to read the numbers on the mailbox. "This is it."

She put the car into gear again and turned into the driveway. Gravel crunched under the tires as the car rolled to a stop in front of the quaint dollhouselike cottage. White roses climbed up a trellis by the front door, and around the corner of the house Jessica caught a glimpse of windswept pines and the rocky coastline.

"Nice place," she said under her breath, her eyes lighting up with speculation. "I guess it won't be so bad."

Just as she climbed out of the convertible, the front door of the house opened, and a small blond girl poked her head out.

"Are you Jessica?" the little girl piped eagerly. Feathery gold ringlets bobbed past her shoulders, and her huge brown eyes were wide with excitement. She wore yellow corduroy overalls and a pink T-shirt, and her bare toes peeked out from under turned-up cuffs.

"That's right," Jessica replied with a delighted grin. She guessed the girl was about five years old. "Are you Allison Kane?"

Allison nodded, her curls bouncing and swaying. "Alex said I should introduce myself." She had a trace of a lisp but was obviously trying hard to overcome it. She frowned in concentration as she added, "Pleased to meet you, Jeth—Jessica."

Holding back a smile, Jessica allowed Allison to lead her by the hand into the house. It would be a relief to baby-sit for someone who wasn't a little brat. Allison seemed like the sweetest little girl she'd ever seen.

So far, so good, Jessica told herself with satisfaction.

"This is our house," Allison chirped as she dragged Jessica through a cozy, cluttered living room.

Jessica gazed around, making a lightning-quick inspection of the house. Books and piles of sheet music covered most of the surfaces in the living room, and there were musical instruments everywhere. Apparently Alex wasn't the only musician in the family. She paused for a moment, noticing an expensive stereo system. Then Allison tugged on her hand.

"Alex is in the sun-room."

"OK, OK." Jessica followed, and through a pair of french doors she saw a gigantic grand piano. Sheets of music notation paper were spread across the music stand. Beyond the piano were windows looking out across the ocean.

She raised her eyebrows appreciatively. Spending three afternoons a week in this house wouldn't hurt at all! "Nice view," she observed casually, smiling down at Allison.

"Isn't it fantastic? A real source of inspiration," came a warm, low-pitched voice from behind her.

She turned, recognizing Alex Kane's voice from the telephone. But she stopped in her tracks when she saw him. For a long, heart-fluttering moment, she couldn't think of a thing to say. Alex was undoubtedly one of the best-looking guys she had ever seen. The same soft blond hair that framed his sister's pixie face curled behind his ears like gold silk, and intelligence and sensitivity sparkled in his eyes.

"Hi, Jessica. Thanks for coming," he said warmly, walking toward her with his hand outstretched. "I really appreciate your helping me out this way."

Staring into his deep brown eyes, she shook his hand mechanically.

"I see you've already made Allison's acquaintance," he drawled, smiling down adoringly at his sister.

Suddenly the thing Jessica wanted most was for Alex Kane to look at *her* like that. Here was a gorgeous college student who was sensitive and creative and devastatingly handsome. Instantly Jessica pulled herself together and began to plan her strategy.

"We met outside," she replied, giving him her most brilliant smile. Behind her poised facade, her mind was racing, trying to decide the best tactics to use. The grand piano, and the fact that he was a composer and a music student, gave her a cue: She was now a dedicated music-lover.

"You have so many wonderful instruments," she said, turning and gesturing at the violin on a chair, the gleaming silver flute on the piano, and the guitar leaning against the wall.

"Do you like music?" A heart-melting smile lit up his face, and he seemed to regard her in a new light.

"Oh, yes," Jessica gushed. "I couldn't live without music in my life. It's—it's—" She broke off and shrugged. For a moment she contemplated saying something about it being more important than food, but she knew that was pushing it. "There's no way to describe it," she concluded with a modest smile.

Alex beamed at her. "I'm really glad to hear you say that. Music is my life, obviously. Our whole family plays." They wandered into the sun-room. Alex tousled Allison's hair and added, "And this little performer is getting pretty good, too."

Jessica looked at Allison in surprise. "What do you play, Allison?"

"Recorder. Wanna hear me?"

"Sure!" The smile remained fixed on Jessica's face, but inside she was wondering about Allison's answer. A recorder was some kind of a flute, wasn't it?

"Why don't you play for Jessica outside, huh?" Alex suggested with an indulgent smile.

"OK, Alex." Allison ran over to a shelf, got her recorder, then took Jessica's hand trustingly and led her toward the sliding glass door. "Let's go out on the beach."

Actually, I'd rather stay here with your brother, Jessica wanted to say, even though she thought Allison was a sweetheart.

"Good idea. I need a few uninterrupted hours to work on this symphony," Alex Kane explained in an undertone as he looked into Jessica's eyes. "It means a lot to me that there's someone here to keep an eye on her when she gets home from kindergarten—and keep her quiet, too!"

Jessica's heart flip-flopped before she broke eye contact with him. "Sure," she replied meaningfully. She raised her eyes to his again and added, "I think I know what you mean."

He smiled and headed for the piano. "That's great, Jessica. Thanks a lot. Have fun outside, Allison."

Jessica felt an impatient tug on her hand, so she let Allison pull her outdoors.

Outside, they trudged through the hot sand several yards away from the small house. Jessica sank gratefully to the ground and crossed her legs while Allison knelt by her side, chattering happily. Jessica narrowed her eyes against the glare and surveyed the bungalow, plotting her strategy. She had gone after college men before—with limited success. But this time she was determined to make it work.

"Should I play 'Jolly Miller' or 'Greensleeves'?"

"Huh? Oh," Jessica muttered, startled out of her reverie. Allison was looking at her so hopefully, she felt her heart melt. And Jessica didn't usually have any patience with small children. "Which is your favorite?"

Allison frowned seriously, then said, " 'Greensleeves.' "

"Go ahead, then." Jessica folded her arms and prepared to pretend to look very impressed. How good could a kindergartener be?

Allison put the recorder to her lips and began to play a haunting melody. Her chubby little fingers barely covered the holes, but she played the simple tune perfectly, drawing huge breaths every now and then.

Stunned, Jessica stared at the little girl's solemn brown eyes. She was *good*!

"That was terrific!" she exclaimed as Allison finished. Chewing on her lower lip, Jessica studied the little girl's recorder. It had to be an extremely simple instrument to learn, or else how could a child play it? And if a child could play it, Jessica Wakefield certainly could.

"I bet your brother thinks you're pretty special, too, huh?" Jessica teased gently.

Allison gave her a shy nod, squirming up onto her knees in the sand. "Alex says music is the most wonderful thing in the whole *universe*!"

"And I bet he thinks people who play music are pretty wonderful, too!"

Allison nodded again, her gentle brown eyes aglow. "Do you play music, Jessica?"

"Are you kidding? I've been playing music since—since I was your age," Jessica assured her. She counted on Allison passing the information along to Alex. Jessica felt a twinge of guilt about lying, but it was all for a good cause, she told herself. "Now play something else for me—I really want to hear you."

With an eager smile Allison settled down on the sand to play her entire repertoire. Listening with half her attention, Jessica turned her eyes back to the bungalow. Through the big patio doors she could see Alex playing the piano and jotting down notes on paper. His face was serious and intent as he concentrated on his music.

Obviously the way to this man's heart was through music, she reasoned. So it was equally obvious that although she had no ear for music, sang off-key, and had never wanted to learn to play an instrument, Jessica had to become a serious musician. It was as simple as that.

"Jessica? Can we look for shells?"

"What? Oh, sure, Allison." Flashing a brilliant smile, Jessica stood up and held out her hand for the little girl to take. She gave Allison's recorder a speculative glance. It looked so easy! That was what she would do. She'd get herself a recorder, an instruction book, and by the end of the week, she'd be a virtuoso. No problem.

"Let's go," Jessica said, feeling a glow of satisfaction spread through her. It was great to solve a problem so easily. Now all she had to do was put it into action. She cast one last look over her shoulder at the house and gave herself a silent salute.

Jessica Wakefield, you're a genius.

Three

Shrugging into a denim jacket, Robin Wilson ran down the front steps of her house and climbed into George Warren's light blue GTO.

"Hi," she said, yanking the door shut after her.

George leaned across to kiss her tenderly on the lips. "How's it going?"

A brief, nervous smile passed across her face, and she turned her eyes away from his. His calm gray eyes always seemed to see too much. "Fine," she said hastily. Her conversation with Annie at lunchtime came back to her, nagging at her conscience. She had to tell him about being accepted to Sarah Lawrence. But not yet.

"Is the Dairi Burger OK?" he asked, looking over his shoulder as he backed down the driveway. The lopsided grin he gave her added a special charm to his lean, handsome face. "You know college guys like me are real big spenders." George was a freshman at Sweet Valley College.

"Fine. The Dairi Burger is fine," she assured him without smiling. Usually Robin enjoyed George's quirky sense of humor. He would always make fun of himself rather than another person because he hated to hurt anyone's feelings. In fact, when Enid Rollins had been partially paralyzed due to an accident for which George felt responsible, he almost hadn't been able to break up with her to go out with Robin. He thought it would hurt Enid too much on top of the terrible trauma she was going through.

And even though Robin had been heartsick at the thought that they couldn't be together, she couldn't help loving him even more for his sensitivity. What she was afraid of now was that he was so sensitive he might react badly when she told him about college.

"OK—listen, I was thinking," he went on happily, turning the car in the direction of the popular hamburger place. "Maybe this weekend we could rent a plane and fly along the coast—look for sunken wrecks from the air." Robin and George had met while taking flying lessons, and they tried to fly together as often as possible.

Robin stared absently out the window, not really seeing the tree-lined streets of Sweet Valley. "Oh, OK—no, wait a second. I have to practice my diving this weekend," she said with an apologetic smile.

"Well . . . we'll see, OK?"

She nodded and looked out the window again, her mind far away from both airplanes and diving. "Sure."

Tell him. Tell him now, she commanded herself sternly.

"Uh, George? I was—I've been thinking about college," she began in a rush. If she just got it out quickly, it would all be over with. "I was thinking about, you know—where I'd want to go."

"That's easy," George replied with a carefree laugh. "UCLA is a natural for you. It's got a great computer science department, you can dive all year, and last but not least you won't be too far from me." He finished up with a shrug and a good-natured grin. "What more could you want?"

"Nothing," she admitted lamely. "It's just that—"

"That what! I don't see why it's such a big deal." George pulled the car into the Dairi Burger parking lot and gave her a reassuring smile.

Robin fidgeted with a button on her jacket.

She could feel her cheeks burning. George was so confident that things would work out perfectly. He had everything planned out. If she told him now, he'd be crushed. He might even take it personally, thinking that applying to a school in the East meant she didn't love him anymore.

"Well, see—I'm worried about how I'm going to pay for it," she explained truthfully. Her parents were divorced, and neither of them made very much money. The only luxuries she and her mother enjoyed were the ones Aunt Fiona lavished on them. Money was a serious problem as far as college was concerned.

George touched her cheek with one gentle hand and turned her to face him. "Is that all?" he asked with a tender smile. "Don't worry about it. You can always get a student loan or a scholarship—or how about that rich aunt of yours who's always helping out?"

A fiery blush swept up Robin's cheeks as she met George's gaze. Carefully, not wanting to hurt his feelings, she pulled away and looked down at her lap again. "Well, the problem with her is . . . there are always strings attached whenever Aunt Fiona gives us anything. She—she'd expect something in return."

"Geez." George shook his head. "Listen, Robin. I know you and your mom really count on her, but she has no right to make decisions for you. I mean, if she wants to help out, let her help, but don't let her manipulate you into something you don't want to do."

Robin nodded mutely. She really wasn't sure how to answer him. Was it wrong for her aunt to put conditions on her offer, or was it perfectly natural and understandable? Was she, Robin, just being a selfish brat about it all? It was difficult to know what was right.

"And besides," he added with a slightly sarcastic laugh, "what's she going to do? Tell you where to go to school?"

She raised her eyes. This was her chance to tell him. George *would* understand, she decided. He was always so generous and sympathetic. Opening her mouth, she began, "Well, actually—"

"Robin, listen," George cut her off, looking intently into her eyes. "We both know you want to go to school here in California. We'll work out a way for you to do that. Don't worry. We'll figure something out."

She let her breath out slowly. She couldn't do it.

Smiling, George put one arm across her shoulders and pulled her to him. "I love you, Robin. I'll stand by you and help you out."

Even if I decide to go to school in New York?

Robin asked silently. She focused her eyes on George's knees, feeling the gentle pressure of his arm around her. *Why is it so hard to tell him?* she wondered. *And why does it have to be so hard to decide?*

"So anyway, I told Lila that was the most ridiculous thing I'd ever heard of."

Elizabeth chuckled and ran water over a dirty serving dish. As she leaned down to put it in the dishwasher, her eyes fell on Prince Albert, the Wakefields' golden retriever, who was sitting by the kitchen door. He met her affectionate glance and thumped his tail on the floor. Faint sounds from the television drifted in from the living room, where Mr. and Mrs. Wakefield were watching the evening news.

"I don't see why going to the movies with her father's friend's son is so ridiculous," Elizabeth commented to her twin. Jessica handed her the dishwashing detergent silently. "What's wrong with it?"

Jessica rolled her eyes. "He's only *fifteen*, that's what's wrong with it," she replied, her voice resonating with indignant horror.

"Oh, definitely ridiculous, then," Elizabeth said lightly. She tried not to smile. Glancing at the sinkful of dirty pots and pans, she added, "Are you planning to help with these, by the way?"

With a look of offended dignity, Jessica said, "Of course I am. How can—"

The phone rang, cutting her off. Eyes alight with anticipation, Jessica made a dash for the kitchen phone. "It's Lila," she said gleefully.

Sighing, Elizabeth turned back to the sink. She was tempted to leave half the dishes for Jessica to do whenever she got off the phone, which might not be for hours, in light of Jessica and Lila's track record for marathon phone calls. Elizabeth shrugged and pushed up her sleeves.

"I'm telling you, Lila"—Jessica perched on the kitchen table and twirled the phone cord around one finger—"I nearly *died* when I saw him. . . . Ha, ha, very funny. No, seriously, he's *gorgeous*. . . . Yeah . . . yeah—"

At the sink Elizabeth shook her head and soaped up the wok. Jessica was always finding gorgeous boys and having tremendous crushes on them. The next thing Elizabeth expected to overhear was how her twin was planning to snap this one up.

"Yes," Jessica declared seriously. "I think so. . . . No, no girlfriend that I found out about. Anyway, so he's this composer, right? A music student at State. . . . I know, I know. But—see, what I'm going to do is learn how to play the recorder—the *recorder*. Lila, don't you know anything? It's the simplest thing in the world. His little sister plays it—"

Amazed, Elizabeth turned to look at her twin. "You don't know a thing about music!" she exclaimed. Jessica quieted her impatiently with one hand.

"Right." Jessica continued her conversation with Lila. "And he'll be floored. I figure he'll probably write a symphony for me someday or something," she said airily, crossing her legs and bobbing one foot up and down as she examined her fingernails. She let out a peal of laughter at something Lila said. "No, are you crazy? I know—but I'll try to get him into something a little more mainstream."

Jessica glanced across the kitchen and covered the mouthpiece with one hand. "I'll do those, Lizzie!"

"Yeah, right," Elizabeth muttered affectionately as she rinsed off the last pan. Sometimes she felt that living with her impetuous twin was like being part of a soap opera!

"OK—right. OK, but . . . tomorrow, Lila . . . *definitely!* Bye!"

Sighing in satisfaction, Jessica jumped down from the table and bounced over to her sister. "Hey, you're all finished," she scolded in a mock angry tone. She wagged one finger at Elizabeth. "I told you I'd do them."

Elizabeth looked at her twin for a long moment. Between her manhunting schemes and her carefully orchestrated ploys for getting out of chores, Jessica was a constant source of fascination. "Well, if you want, I could get them all dirty again, and then you could wash them."

"Forget it." Jessica gave her sister an arch smile. "I can't help it if Lila calls at a bad time, can I?"

Grimacing, Elizabeth shook her head. "I wouldn't be surprised if you tell Lila exactly when to call every night so you can get out of the dishes."

"I don't," her twin replied. "But that sure is a good idea!"

After cheerleading practice the next day, Jessica hustled Cara Walker, one of her best friends, into the Fiat with her. "I wish you could meet him," she gushed, looking in the rearview mirror as she pulled out of the parking lot. "You'd instantly fall out of love with Steven."

Cara grinned and tossed back her dark hair. She had been dating Steven Wakefield in a serious way for months, and despite the fact that Jessica had conspired to get the two of them together, Cara knew she hated the thought of anyone being "trapped" in a long-term relationship. "Don't count on it," she said wryly.

Within a few minutes they were parked in a space at the Valley Mall. Jessica and Cara grabbed their bags and headed for the music store.

"What is a recorder, anyway?" Cara asked as they shouldered their way through the crowded mall atrium.

"Kind of like a flute—at least, it sort of sounds like one, but it looks different. Come on." Taking Cara's arm, Jessica entered a music store. "I'd like to buy a recorder," she announced to the woman behind the counter.

"Well, that's nice. Bass, tenor, alto, soprano, sopranino?"

Jessica looked blankly at Cara. Her friend shrugged.

"Uh . . ." Thinking about Monday afternoon, Jessica called up a picture of Allison's recorder. "The usual kind—you know, about this long?" she asked, gesturing with both hands.

The woman smiled doubtfully. "An alto?"

"Right."

"Fine. Wood or plastic?"

Jessica closed her eyes briefly. Who would have thought she'd have to go through such an interrogation just to buy a little flute? "Does it matter?"

Cara suppressed a snort of laughter. "Your love of music is really showing, Jess."

"Well, how much were you planning to spend? We have a lovely alto in pearwood for three hundred dollars."

Jessica's jaw dropped. She stared at her friend in horror. "Can you wait a minute?" she asked the saleswoman as she steered Cara away by the elbow. "What am I going to do?" she whispered frantically.

"You don't really want to spend three hundred dollars just to impress this guy, do you?" Cara asked skeptically.

"No, of course not!"

The saleswoman cleared her throat. "We also have some plastic recorders for eleven ninety-five."

"Fine—I'll take one of those." Jessica gasped with relief. She gave Cara a triumphant look. Cara turned away to hide her grin.

"And some music, too. Some nice classical stuff," she added.

"Maybe you'd like to start with a basic instruction manual," the woman suggested, raising her eyebrows.

She reached up on a shelf and brought down three slim spiral-bound books. "One of these might be a good way to start."

Jessica flipped through them impatiently. They looked like a lot of dull exercises, but she was confident she could skip those and get right to the good stuff. "Sure. That's fine. I'll take this one," she decided, choosing one at random.

As the saleswoman rang up her purchase, Jessica leaned one elbow on the glass counter and gave Cara a knowing smile. "This is great—I bet you by the end of the week I'll be playing Mozart."

"And you'll have that guy eating out of your hand."

Jessica grinned and then wiggled her eye-brows up and down. "Of course!"

Elizabeth waved to Jeffrey as he drove off. Then she turned to head for the front door of the Wakefields' attractive split-level house. They had spent the afternoon at the public library. Elizabeth was getting research material for a history paper she was working on, and Jeffrey had accompanied her. However, they had spent as much time talking and gazing into each other's eyes as they had looking for research material.

She grinned as she let herself in the front door. Maybe they hadn't gotten much work done, but they'd had a good time! As she walked up the stairs to her room, she heard a shrill piping. Puzzled, she quickened her pace and opened the door to Jessica's room.

The Hershey Bar—the family nickname for Jessica's room since the time she had painted the walls dark brown on a whim—was in its usual messy state, with clothes and papers and books spread around haphazardly. A soda can was perched on the stereo, and the window was propped open with a shoe. Planted cross-legged on her unmade bed, a red-faced Jessica was scowling at a book opened in front of her. She clutched a brown recorder in her left hand.

"Hi, Jess."

Jessica looked up, frowning. "Hi," she muttered, dropping her eyes to the music book again. Grimacing, she placed the recorder in her mouth, aligned her fingers on the holes, and blew. A feeble, wavering whistle came out of the instrument.

"Teaching yourself the recorder, huh?"

With another frustrated glare at her recorder, Jessica nodded. "I can't make it sound right, though."

Elizabeth shrugged. "Do you think you bought a broken one or something?" she asked, coming in and sitting next to her sister. She leaned over to examine the instruction book. The open page showed a fingering diagram and several bars of notes.

"No—I don't know." Jessica blew forcefully into it again and produced a shrill squeak. "Here, you try it. See if you can make it work."

Elizabeth raised both hands. "I don't know how to play it, Jess. Don't ask me." But she looked curiously at the instrument and at the fingering diagram. She had once heard two girls playing recorder duets on the beach, and the music had been hauntingly beautiful. "Well . . . OK—let me try."

Taking the recorder, Elizabeth carefully fitted her fingers over the holes and blew. A light, airy note came out, steady and true. She handed the recorder back to her sister. "Maybe you were blowing too hard."

"Maybe," Jessica grumbled.

Jessica tried again to produce a single clear note. Thoughtful, Elizabeth watched her twin. Having the recorder in her hands and playing that one note had been fun—and strangely exciting, too, in a way. For some reason, she had never considered taking up an instrument before. But now, playing the recorder seemed like something she could really enjoy. Her thoughts returned to the girls she had heard on the beach. *Making music like that must be wonderful.*

But it was Jessica's idea, she reminded herself. Often, in the past, Elizabeth had excelled at something that Jessica had failed at. And even though Jessica dropped hobbies easily enough, Elizabeth knew her twin was sometimes hurt that she had "taken over" something of Jessica's. And Elizabeth knew enough not to barge in on her sister's interests again. There were plenty of things in the world for each of them.

If Jessica wanted to play the recorder, then

Elizabeth wasn't even going to think about it. She put her hand on Jessica's shoulder and squeezed.

"Keep trying, Jess. It just takes practice. I bet you'll really be good soon."

Nodding impatiently, Jessica riffled the pages of her lesson book to the back and tried a more difficult fingering. Again she produced a thin squeak that suddenly jumped a whole octave.

Elizabeth let herself out. If learning to play the recorder was what Jessica wanted to do, Elizabeth wasn't going to interfere.

Four

Elizabeth hummed a melody to herself as she ran her finger along the spines of the encyclopedias on Wednesday afternoon. Then, remembering she was in the public library, she stopped and cast a quick guilty look around. The librarian smiled and raised a finger to her lips.

Feeling self-conscious, Elizabeth turned back to the reference books. When she had started her research the day before, she, with Jeffrey there, hadn't accomplished much! But her history report wasn't going to write itself. Elizabeth pulled three volumes off the shelf and cradled them in her arms.

Across the low shelf of encyclopedias, she glimpsed a few of her classmates working on reports and homework. The junior class clown,

Winston Egbert, was whispering something to his girlfriend, Maria Santelli, and she was giggling. At another table Bill Chase was sitting with his perpetually sunburned nose buried in the latest edition of *Surfing Today*. Caroline Pearce was looking up something in a huge atlas and taking notes on a legal pad while Sally Larson looked over her shoulder.

"Liz, hi!"

Elizabeth turned at the sound of her name. George Warren was striding toward her. "Hey, George. How's it going?"

There was a time when Elizabeth couldn't talk to George without a wave of embarrassment flooding through her. That was while he was breaking up with Enid, who was her best friend. Elizabeth had found out about George and Robin before Enid did, which put a terrible strain on their friendship. But that was a long time ago now, and she could admit to herself that George was a really nice guy.

George swung his denim jacket back over one shoulder. "OK—how about you?" He eyed her stack of encyclopedias and grinned. "Writing a paper?"

"Yeah," Elizabeth replied. "So, what brings you here?"

"I'm picking up some books Robin said she needed."

Elizabeth broke into a smile and shifted her books to a more comfortable position. "Listen," she began warmly, putting one hand on George's arm, "I really think it's fantastic about Robin."

"Fantastic?" he repeated with a faintly puzzled look in his eyes.

"Sure—about being accepted early admission to Sarah Lawrence College." Elizabeth faltered to a stop, alarmed by the expression on George's face. Color flooded his cheeks and then washed away, leaving his face pale. With a sick sensation growing in her stomach, Elizabeth realized that George hadn't heard the news about Robin.

One hand flew up to cover her mouth, and her eyes widened. "Oh, no, did I just say something incredibly stupid?"

George's jaw clenched, and he turned his head to one side, staring off across the library. He shook his head slowly. "I guess I'm the stupid one," he whispered.

"I—I didn't mean—I mean, I didn't know—" In an agony of embarrassment, Elizabeth stumbled over her words. She felt terrible!

"I'll see you around," George said in a flat tone. Without looking at her, he hurried away.

Elizabeth stood rooted to the spot, staring dismally at his retreating figure. She closed her eyes briefly and wished she could take back what she had said to George. If Robin hadn't told him about her plans, it wasn't just an oversight. Clearly George wasn't supposed to know. And now he did.

As she put the encyclopedias down on a table, she shook her head. All she could do was hope it wasn't too drastic a mistake.

After an hour of concentrated note-taking, Elizabeth rubbed her eyes wearily and sat back in her chair. The hushed stillness of the library was beginning to get to her, and she felt terrible about letting out Robin's secret. She snapped the heavy volumes shut and then returned them to their shelves. In a few moments she was on her way home.

Prince Albert was home alone when she got there, and even though he gave her a boisterous welcome, Elizabeth wished there were someone to talk to. Jessica was at her baby-sitting job, and Mrs. Wakefield, an interior designer, was at work. Feeling restless, Elizabeth wandered upstairs and peeked into her twin's room.

Smiling at the mess, Elizabeth walked in and picked up some of Jessica's clothes and folded them over one arm. Lost in thought, she sat down on the edge of the bed. There was a hard lump under the covers. Elizabeth reached underneath her and pulled out Jessica's recorder.

Elizabeth stared at it for a long moment. Then, holding it carefully, she blew into the instrument and changed her fingers over the holes. An aimless melody piped into the silent room. She tried a few more notes, attempting to keep each tone pure and steady and even. Her interest aroused, she searched for the lesson book. It was under the bed.

"I know, I know," she muttered as Prince Albert padded into the room and gave her neck an inquisitive sniff. She was hanging over the bed, reaching for the manual. "I'm not really playing it—just trying it out."

She sat up again with the spiral-bound instruction manual in her hand and flipped it open to the first page. The guide demonstrated how to play an E. She duplicated the fingering and played the note easily. With a smile she turned the page, and her thoughts drifted to Julie Porter.

When Elizabeth was in sixth grade, Julie Porter had been one of her best friends. Julie's entire family was musical, and the Porter home always echoed with music from one room or another. At the time Julie was learning the flute, and Elizabeth could remember spending afternoons at Julie's reading a book while her friend practiced. Why she had never taken any music lessons herself she didn't know.

"I should talk to Julie about recorder music," she told herself and adjusted her fingers on the holes again.

But then she quickly closed the book. She had made a promise to herself not to spoil Jessica's new hobby by doing it, too. Feeling a pang of regret, Elizabeth slipped the recorder under the covers and dropped the book back onto the floor.

Forget it, she thought as she pushed herself up off the bed and walked out of the room. It was Jessica's idea to learn to play the recorder, and Elizabeth wasn't going to interfere at all.

"Here you go," Mrs. Wilson said as she handed Robin a dripping plate.

Robin took it silently and wiped it dry, her thoughts far away.

"I think I'll have Alice Wakefield design the new kitchen," her mother continued, rinsing another plate. With a sigh, she shook her head and wiped a dab of soapsuds off her plump wrist. "I'll be so happy when we can get this room remodeled. Honestly, it's so inconvenient and cramped in here." She handed Robin the rinsed plate.

Frowning, Robin dried mechanically and gave her mother an absent nod. Complaining about how awkward and primitive their kitchen was seemed to be one of her mother's favorite pastimes.

"And especially the way your brothers eat! I swear, two dirty cereal bowls and some empty glasses and this place is overflowing!" Mrs. Wilson said with a chuckle. The Wilson boys, Troy, in eighth grade, and Adam, in ninth grade, were at a stage where they seemed to live in front of the refrigerator.

"I've waited a long time for this," she went on. "And now Fiona's finally come through for me. Ooooh! What a relief!" Mrs. Wilson laughed. "It'll be nice to have a dishwasher after all this time."

Robin swallowed hard and cleared her throat. She knew she was taking a big risk by telling her mother what was on her mind, but she had to do it. "Mom?" she began.

"Yes, honey? Hand me that frying pan, would you?"

"Mom, I was thinking. Do you think Aunt Fiona would be upset if I decided I didn't want to go to Sarah Lawrence?"

Her mother let out a frustrated cry as the faucet spurted water at her. She darted Robin a reproving look and reached for a dish towel. "What on earth are you talking about, Robin? Your aunt is sending you to Sarah Lawrence and that's that!"

"But, Mom—" Robin paused and drew a deep breath to steady herself. "Mom, I just haven't been able to make up my mind yet."

Shaking her head, Mrs. Wilson began scrubbing the frying pan with vigorous strokes. "I think it's ridiculous for you to start hemming and hawing about it now—and we're finally getting our new kitchen because Fiona is so pleased about sending you to her old school. If you didn't want to go, you should have said something in the first place."

"But maybe I do want to go, Mom! I'm just not really sure yet!"

"Well, I know it's scary to go so far away, honey," Mrs. Wilson agreed. "But really, I can't understand how you can be unsure about going at all! Your aunt has always been so generous to us—I don't know what we'd do without her! Is it so much to ask to go to a school that will make her happy?"

Robin met her mother's eyes and felt hurt and confusion rippling through her. Didn't her own happiness matter? Or wasn't she allowed to take that into consideration? She felt tears prick her eyes and turned away quickly.

"And what possible reason could you have for turning down such an incredibly generous offer, may I ask?" Mrs. Wilson went on, her irritation becoming clear in her voice.

Keeping her face averted, Robin said in a low voice, "I thought I might want to stay in California—for—for diving, and because of George."

"Oh, Robin!" Mrs. Wilson turned back to the sink and began clattering silverware around. "How can you be so selfish and immature?" she demanded, her voice throbbing with intensity. "I'm really surprised at you. I always thought you were more responsible and grown-up than that."

Stung, Robin bit her lip to keep from crying. She didn't know what to think. She was getting more confused each time the subject came up.

I'm not being immature, am I? Robin asked herself silently. *I just haven't made up my mind yet!*

From the corner of her eye she saw her mother grit her teeth as she tried to shut a cupboard door that always stuck. In a flash Robin realized that she was being sacrificed for a new kitchen! All her mother cared about was getting her kitchen remodeled, and the price was making Robin go to college in New York!

The ironic thing about it was that Robin still thought it would be great to go to Sarah Lawrence College. If it weren't for all the other things in her life, she would jump at her aunt's offer. Over the years Robin had heard lots of her aunt's stories about the school's exciting intellectual and cultural atmosphere. Sarah Lawrence was an excellent school, and it was close to New York City, with its theaters and museums and stores. Spending four years on the East Coast would be a fantastic adventure.

And on top of that, Robin admitted as she glanced around the small, dark kitchen, she couldn't blame her mother for wanting to remodel the room. For the last week Mrs. Wilson had been in a flurry of excitement, poring over catalogs and brochures. Robin's mother had spent so many years making do, scrimping and saving after the divorce and struggling to raise three kids decently. And now she had a chance for something really nice. No wonder she was upset because Robin wasn't sure!

Robin's head spun with conflicting emotions: guilt, anger, gratitude, resentment. It was so difficult to think straight! But there was one thing Robin was sure of. Even though there were plenty of good reasons why she should accept her aunt's generosity, there *were* other considerations in her life. She couldn't just ignore them when it was time to make her decision. She had to approach this problem rationally, and with a level head.

"Mom, I wish you would see it my way—" Robin began on a calmer note.

Mrs. Wilson interrupted her swiftly, her plump cheeks flushing with emotion. "All I see is that my older sister, who has been more than generous to us over the years, is willing to send you to a very expensive college for four years! That's *all* I can see, Robin. I don't see anyone else making the same offer!"

Robin was speechless. There was no way to argue with *that*.

"And another thing," her mother added, her voice sounding strained and tired. "Fiona will be coming to see us next week. She has an opening at a gallery in L.A., and she'll be staying with us for a few days."

The words froze Robin. *Aunt Fiona. Coming here.* If her mother was hard to reason with, her aunt was impossible! Suddenly Robin felt as if time were running out.

"And I hope, Robin, that by the time she gets here, you'll be able to tell her how grateful and happy you are to be going to Sarah Lawrence next year!"

Robin tried once more. "Mom—"

Mrs. Wilson gave her a hard stare, then clamped her lips and turned away.

Her eyes stinging, Robin stalked out of the kitchen. She was beginning to get sick of the word *grateful.* She was beginning to wish her aunt had never offered to send her to college at all.

Five

Her eyes blinded by unshed tears, Robin paused in the front hall and leaned against the windowsill for support. A blurry, moving form took shape out in the driveway. It was George's car, just pulling in. They had been planning to spend the evening at Robin's house. But that was impossible the way things were at the moment. Without stopping to think, Robin grabbed her jacket and ran out into the driveway.

"Let's go somewhere," she choked, slamming the door after her. She was too upset even to look at George and say hello. "I've got to get out of the house."

Silent, George backed out onto the street and turned the car around. They shot forward on a surge of power.

In the corner Robin sat huddled in misery, staring out of the window at the houses and trees flashing by. *It's not fair. It's not fair,* she thought over and over. Her mother was asking so much of her and giving her so little time! And Robin needed time to make the right decision.

The problem was, there were so many factors involved, and she had to weigh *all* of them. On the one hand, she had always wanted to visit New York, but on the other hand, she loved California. On the one hand, Sarah Lawrence had an excellent reputation, but on the other hand, the best computer departments were at the West Coast schools. On the one hand . . . Squeezing her eyes shut, Robin forced herself to calm down and think of something else.

Diving. The diving championship. It was only a week and a half away now. More than anything else, even more than physical conditioning, she had to be mentally prepared for the meet. "If you *believe* you can win, you *can* win," her coach had told her again and again. She had to concentrate her whole mind and spirit on her performance next Sunday. But every time she tried, all her anxieties about her aunt, the new kitchen, her schoolwork, Sarah Lawrence, and George came to the surface.

She looked out the window and noticed they

were driving up the road to Miller's Point. Her eyes flicked back to George's profile, and she frowned. He appeared angry about something, and so far he hadn't said a word.

"George?" The car rolled to a stop. He said nothing and switched off the engine. "George? Is something wrong?"

There was a heavy pause, like the quiet before a thunderstorm. Then George exploded. *"Wrong?"* he repeated, his eyes blazing as he turned to her. "I just found out my girlfriend wants to break up but won't actually tell me! That's what's *wrong*!"

Stunned, Robin stared back at him, her mouth open. "What? What are you talking about? I don't want to break up with you!" she gasped.

"No?" George's voice was icy with sarcasm. "You're just going off to New York without saying anything about it. Were you planning to write me a letter or something?"

Her heart was thundering in her ears, and she could feel her face flushing hot and then cold. She pressed shaking hands against her cheeks. "Who—who told you that?"

"What difference does it make? I know you're going to Sarah Lawrence, and I know you never said anything about it to me. I'm not stupid, Robin. I can take a hint."

"I didn't mean—George!" Robin clenched her

hands into fists and squeezed them between her knees. She couldn't think straight—she couldn't find the right words. But the look of pain and hurt on George's face forced the words out of her. "I didn't tell you yet because I thought you would be hurt and that you wouldn't understand," she faltered, love and sincerity in every painful syllable.

"You're right. I am, and I don't." George was scowling out the window, his face turned from her. But she could see his jaw tightening.

"My aunt said she'd pay for college if I went to the same school she did, and my guidance counselor said I qualified for early admission, and she thought I should try for it—and they accepted me. But I'm not sure if I want to go. . . ."

George was stubbornly silent.

"Because I thought I might want to stay here and be near you and keep diving and—" The strain was too much. Robin burst into tears. "And—and I can't make up my mind what I sh-should do," she wailed, hiccuping and pressing her hands over her mouth. She glanced forlornly at George, wishing he would just take her in his arms and comfort her, help her do the right thing. But he just kept looking out the window.

Robin caught her breath on a sob, trying to

bring her emotions under control. *What a disaster!* she thought. *This wasn't the way I wanted to tell him at all!*

But she couldn't understand how he had found out. So far, no one knew except Annie—and Jessica. But Jessica and George weren't friends. There wouldn't be any reason for Jessica to see or talk to George. So it had to have been Annie. Annie had betrayed her confidence, even after Robin had made it clear how important it was that she tell George herself.

At the realization, a fresh wave of hurt and confusion coursed through Robin. She shook her head in despair and wiped futilely at her tears. It was too much. She felt as though she might scream with everything that she suddenly had to deal with.

"Well? *Are* you going?"

She looked at George quickly. She was relieved that he was speaking to her at last, but she was still terribly confused. She shook her head. "I don't know," she whispered after a moment. "I don't know what I should do."

"I think it's pretty obvious," George said, keeping his voice low as he turned to look through the windshield again. He pounded the steering wheel. "I can't *believe* you're even thinking about going!"

"But it's a really good school!" Robin heard the

pleading tone in her voice and hated herself for it. She sounded so weak and whiny. "And my aunt will pay for it *all* if I go there!"

"Well, why can't she pay for a school here in California?"

Robin shrugged, helpless. "She just won't. That's the way she is. Sarah Lawrence is sort of a family tradition. She doesn't want me going someplace else."

"Listen, Robin." George turned to her and put his hands on her shoulders. His gaze was searching. "Just tell her you don't need her handouts. Tell her you don't want to go!"

But maybe I do want to, Robin replied silently. She dropped her eyes. George just didn't understand what an opportunity this was, what a chance for something good and valuable. All he could see was that she might be leaving California—leaving him.

If only she could explain what going to Sarah Lawrence could mean. Just going to college early would be an exciting challenge, and in a place like Sarah Lawrence it could be even better. And being on her own, able to make her own decisions, was something Robin looked forward to, even though it was a little scary.

But the thought of going to the college in California, where her roots were, where George was, was also exciting.

Sighing heavily, Robin leaned forward to rest her head on George's shoulder. Echoing her sigh, he wrapped his arms around her and held her tight. Robin closed her eyes wearily.

I wish I didn't have to decide. She felt a childish impulse to stamp her feet and refuse. But she knew she had to face facts like an adult. The problem wasn't just going to disappear. It was a decision she had to reach all by herself, too, because no one seemed to want to help her out. And it seemed that no matter what she chose, someone was going to be hurt and disappointed.

Jessica pulled her hair back into a ponytail, then plopped down on the grass across from Cara. Silently she held out her hands, and Cara pulled her forward so she could stretch the backs of her legs. Then Jessica sat up and pulled Cara. On the ground all around them the other cheerleaders were stretching out, too. All except Robin, who hadn't arrived yet.

"I'm telling you, Cara, this guy is it," Jessica declared. "I can feel it."

Cara grunted as she bounced her forehead down on her knees. Her dark brown ponytail flipped over her head. "You say that every time."

"No, this time I'm serious," Jessica insisted. She let go of Cara's hands and began twisting at the waist. "Listen to this. Yesterday I was on the beach playing with Allison, and he was standing at the window, just *staring* at me with this expression. . . ." She shivered at the memory.

"Maybe he was looking at his sister," Cara shot back with a teasing grin. "Or the ocean. Ever think of that?"

Jessica shook her head condescendingly. "Oh, *please,* Cara. I think I know when a man is looking at me."

Stifling a giggle, Cara leaned back on her elbows and began doing leg-lifts. She craned her neck so she could still talk to Jessica. "How's the great virtuoso doing with the recor—oh, here comes Robin. Finally."

Rolling over to her side, Jessica cast a glance over her shoulder. Robin was stalking toward them, her face set and stern and her brown eyes snapping with anger. "What's with her?" Jessica wondered aloud. She kept her eyes on her co-captain out of idle curiosity.

Without a word Robin dropped her duffel bag on the ground on the opposite side of the group from Annie Whitman and began her stretches. Annie pushed herself up and trotted over to Robin.

"Hi, Robin," she said, huffing, smiling as she arched backward to limber up some more.

Robin didn't say anything. She just turned her back on Annie and leaned over, grabbing her ankles.

Surprised, Jessica shot Cara a meaningful glance. Cara nodded, and her eyes widened with interest.

"Robin?" Annie repeated, a faint note of puzzlement in her voice. She fluffed her dark curly hair and walked around Robin to stand in front of her. "What's up?"

"I don't want to talk to you." Robin spoke in an undertone and turned away from Annie, but even Jessica could hear the anger.

Annie's face registered stunned confusion. "What? Why?" she demanded, shaking her head in disbelief.

"You know perfectly well why, you traitor!" Whirling around to face Annie, Robin balled her hands into fists at her sides. Her eyes were blazing with anger. "You told George about Sarah Lawrence when you *knew* I hadn't told him yet! He's furious with me, and it's all your fault!"

"I did not!"

"Don't give me that innocent look, Annie Whitman. I know you did—you knew we'd have a fight about it! You probably wanted us to!"

Angry tears spilled down Robin's face, and Annie shook her head in shock. All the other cheerleaders were watching, spellbound, not even pretending they weren't listening to Robin.

"You were probably hoping we'd break up,

right?" Robin stormed on, her shoulders heaving with emotion. "Maybe you even wanted him for yourself!"

Annie opened her mouth in an astonished gasp. "That's not true, and you know it! I don't want your boyfriend, Robin—you're being totally paranoid!" She stared at Robin for another moment, pain and hurt showing clearly in her pretty face. Then she walked rigidly toward her pile of books and her cheerleader's jacket, picked them up, and stalked off the field.

Jessica turned to watch Annie's exit. Then she looked back at Robin again. Then she looked at Cara. *What a scene,* she thought with a silent whistle. Cara nodded slowly, as though reading her mind.

One by one the cheerleaders went back to their stretching exercises. No one said a word. As she waved her arms in quick, tight circles by her sides, Jessica watched Robin.

So, George didn't know—until now. I wonder why Robin didn't tell him? I wonder who did *tell him?*

Then her memory replayed a short conversation with her twin the night before. Elizabeth had mentioned in passing that she had run into George Warren at the library. *Liz must have told him,* she decided. And since she had told Elizabeth, ultimately it was Jessica's own fault.

But, Jessica reminded herself defensively, Robin never said anything about keeping it a secret. How was she supposed to know not to tell anyone about it?

Jessica decided it was really Robin's fault. There was nothing for *her* to feel guilty about.

"Do you know what that was all about?" Cara whispered, jerking her head toward Robin. "That stuff about Sarah Lawrence?"

Jessica lowered her eyes and shrugged noncommittally. "Maybe she wants to go to college in New York, so she and George had a fight about it."

"Oh."

From under her lashes Jessica darted another lightning glance at Robin. Ever since Robin had lost all that weight, she had been serious competition for Jessica. Being beautiful, brainy, making co-captain of the varsity squad, and becoming an excellent diver had made Robin a definite presence in the junior class. In fact, Robin did just about everything well. She had even won the title of Homecoming Queen away from Jessica.

Jessica nodded thoughtfully. If Robin and George broke up and if Robin and Annie weren't friends anymore, there wouldn't be anything to keep Robin in Sweet Valley. And as far as Jessica was concerned, it wouldn't be a very tragic loss. So, all things considered, Jessica didn't think she would set the record straight on who told George. She would just mind her own business and keep her mouth shut.

"OK, let's do some work on the pyramid, you guys," she announced, jumping to her feet. She flashed them all a brilliant smile before she turned to Robin. "Is Annie coming back?"

Robin blushed. "I don't know."

"Maybe I should go ask her what's wrong," Jessica suggested sweetly, taking a step in the direction in which Annie had disappeared.

"Forget it. We can do the pyramid without her." Her jaw set stubbornly, Robin turned away.

Six

Robin tugged down the edges of her bathing suit and stared moodily at the end of the diving board. Beyond, the water of the swimming pool sparkled and rippled in the sunlight. A dark figure rose up from the bottom and broke the surface near the ladder.

"How was that?" Tracy King, Robin's leading competitor, called, flinging water from her short-cropped hair as she hung on the ladder.

Gradually Robin focused on her. "Oh . . . um—OK. It was good."

"Man, you're on another planet today," Tracy said with a snicker. She hauled herself up the ladder and stood dripping on the cement, her hands on her hips. "Go on, let's see you."

Taking a deep breath, Robin turned her eyes

back to the end of the diving board. Lately she felt as if she couldn't get enough air. It was anxiety, she realized, trying to steady her nerves. Here it was already Saturday, and she wasn't any calmer than she had been at the beginning of the week. In fact, she felt even more tense. She paced to the end of the board and stared down into the water with her toes gripping the edge. Then she turned around, shooting her arms out for balance, and pushed up and out.

The instant she plunged into the water, Robin knew it was a terrible dive. Her legs were bent, her hands apart—terrible. With an inward groan, Robin struggled to the surface and swam to the ladder. As she dragged herself up out of the water, she caught the smirk on Tracy's face.

Irritably Robin adjusted one shoulder strap and walked through the puddles to the diving board again. She watched sourly as Tracy climbed up the ladder to the five-meter platform. Tracy was her next-door neighbor, and although they weren't exactly friends, the two girls had a common bond in their diving. Lately, though, the casual spirit of competition between them had been getting more serious. The regional championships coming up had put an edge on their rivalry. Robin planned to win. And she knew perfectly well that Tracy wanted to win, too.

While she watched, Tracy took three long

strides to the end of the board and lifted herself gracefully up into the air in a double-flip. She plunged straight into the water like a bullet. The water closed in over her with hardly a splash.

"Show-off," Robin muttered, leaning against the diving board ladder. She could do that, too, just as cleanly and perfectly. But she knew she couldn't do it today, not with her concentration totally shot.

"Robin, let's go," her coach called as she returned from the pool office. Dina Taylor, an Olympic silver medalist, coached diving at Sweet Valley College, and she also coached the local youth diving program. Under her coaxing and prodding, Robin had progressed quickly to a serious competitive level. It was hard, because being a cheerleader for Sweet Valley High took a lot of her time, too. But Dina kept after her and made her competitive drive sharp.

"Robin?" Dina repeated.

"Yeah?" Robin stared blankly at the coach and then blushed. Rising hastily, she paced to the end of the board for another dive.

Just as she raised her arms Dina interrupted her. "Robin, what do you think you're doing?"

"Huh?" Blushing again, Robin swallowed hard. Dina was looking at her and shaking her head.

Gesturing with one hand, Dina said, "Come here. I want to talk to you."

Robin hugged her arms around herself to keep from shivering and jumped down from the board. Her expression was mournful.

"Listen, Robin. You know the meet is a week from tomorrow, right? If you're not serious about this, don't waste my time."

"I am!"

Dina put one hand on Robin's shoulder and smiled. "What's wrong, then?"

Robin looked away, her eyes on Tracy as the other girl executed a beautiful back-flip with a full twist. She shook her head and looked down at her feet. "It's just that my family thinks I should go to school in New York. . . ."

"What do *you* want to do?"

Shrugging, Robin said, "I—I don't know. I just . . ." Her voice trailed off, and she sighed. "It's so hard to decide."

"Robin, I know this is important to you," her coach said sympathetically. "But this meet is important, too. If you are serious about diving, you have to work and concentrate on next Sunday. Otherwise, you'll never take a first."

Robin nodded mutely. She wanted to take first place. But between now and then, her aunt was going to arrive, and Robin still didn't know how she was going to face her, or what she was going to say. Yes or no?

For the next two hours, Robin tried to banish everything but diving from her mind. But it was impossible, and she ended up blundering through the worst diving practice she could remember. She felt relieved when she saw George arrive to pick her up. Hastily grabbing her towel, she ran into the locker room to change her clothes. In a few minutes she joined him in the pool's parking lot. He was leaning against his car, his arms crossed.

"Hi," she said, feeling slightly nervous as she approached.

He still looked downcast and hurt, but he managed a faint smile. "Hi. How was practice?"

Robin rolled her eyes. "Nauseating."

She smiled, trying to cajole him into a better mood, but he just looked away. Seeing his hurt and bitter expression, Robin felt her heart turn over. She put her arms around him impulsively. She couldn't stand being the cause of his unhappiness. If she just told him she would stay in California, he would be ecstatic.

Maybe I should just stay, Robin told herself. *George will be happy, and I can keep diving all year. I'll think of some way to pay for college. It's the best way.*

She closed her eyes, took a deep breath, and then mumbled into his shoulder. "I—I'm not going to go."

He held her away from him and stared at her. "You're not?"

For a moment Robin felt her heart thudding wildly in her chest. She had done it. It was over with. Nodding, she put her head on his shoulder again and smiled faintly to herself. It was a relief to have it settled, finally. Secretly she was glad that Annie wouldn't be able to get her hooks into George, if that was her plan. Feeling fiercely possessive, Robin hugged her arms around him even tighter and rubbed her cheek on his orange polo shirt. "I'm not leaving you," she whispered.

"I'm so glad," he murmured into her hair. "I knew you wouldn't go. That aunt of yours can't run your life for you."

Robin nodded, her eyes fixed on a tree nearby. Her aunt wasn't going to run her life. No Sarah Lawrence. No money. But she would have her independence. That was worth a lot.

Looks like the state university for me, Robin thought in a detached way. *If I can get enough money even for that.*

"Jessica? Is today Saturday or Sunday?" Allison asked seriously. She squatted in front of Jessica and Lila, her bucket and shovel clutched in her sandy fists.

Jessica rolled over onto one side and caught a grin from Lila. "Saturday. Why?"

"I get them mixed up," Allison admitted shyly. "Watch me make a sand castle?"

"Sure. I'm watching." Jessica watched as Allison trotted a few yards away and began scooping sand into the pail. Then Jessica lay back and squinted at the glaringly bright sky. She wasn't supposed to come on Saturdays, but that weekend Alex's parents were running a conference in San Francisco, and he had asked her to help out. Lila had come along, and they had taken Allison to the local beach.

"She's a pretty decent kid," Lila said. "You really lucked out with her."

"Tell me about it. I also lucked out with the decent kid's brother."

Lila suppressed a snort of laughter. "Yeah, right! Is he madly in love with you yet?"

"Not yet, but he will be," Jessica replied breezily. She propped herself up on one elbow and cast a lazy, surveying glance along the beach. There were lots of Sweet Valley High boys around—John Pfeifer, Tom McKay, Max Dellon, Eddie Roth—all bodysurfing or playing Frisbee. But they were just boys. They couldn't compare to someone as sophisticated and mature as Alex. Jessica gave her friend a serene smile. "I'm working on it, Lila. We're making some definite progress."

Rolling her eyes, Lila reached for the cocoa

butter and began rubbing her legs with it. They were camped out on an old red Oriental rug from Lila's house. It was huge, and Lila needed to find a couple of boys to drag it from the trunk of her car whenever she brought it to the beach. But both girls agreed it had a lot of style.

"So? Give me the details," Lila prompted, tossing the cocoa butter back onto the rug.

Jessica sighed. "Well," she began, her blue-green eyes dancing, "yesterday we had this long talk about this symphony he's composing. I don't know, he was talking about different movements and the scoring—all this stuff I didn't really understand." Jessica paused to catch her breath. "But he thought I knew exactly what he was saying. I'm really good at that. And believe me, he was *really* impressed."

Lila gave her a skeptical grimace.

"And he was looking at me so seriously." She closed her eyes for dramatic impact. "It just gave me the shivers, Lila. I swear. He's so sexy you can't—"

"Jessica? See me? See me?"

She sat up and waved to Allison. "Yeah. That's a great castle, Allison. Make it bigger! Add some more rooms!"

"OK."

As Jessica watched Allison, her mind went back to the recorder she had bought to impress

Alex Kane. She had told him she played it, and he kept asking to hear her, despite her modest protests. Making a sour face, she realized she would have to practice some more.

Unfortunately she was beginning to regret it in a big way. The recorder was a lot harder than she had expected it to be, and on top of that, it seemed a pretty wimpy instrument. You couldn't play any fun songs on it—all the instruction manual had were dumb little folk songs and moldy old English ballads.

"You know, Jess. I think you're making a big mistake going after this guy." Lila's cynical voice broke into Jessica's musings. "You're always falling for these older men, and it never works out."

Jessica gave her friend a withering look and tucked her knees up under her chin. *I'll get him,* she vowed. *I will.*

"Jessica! Allison!"

Startled, Jessica spun around on the rug at the sound of Alex Kane's voice, and she felt her eyes widen. He was striding toward them across the sand in a bathing suit, his legs and chest muscular and tan. His blond hair shone almost white in the brilliant sunshine. As Allison screeched and dashed over to her brother, Alex caught her up in his arms and swung her around in the air. Allison laughed ecstatically.

Jessica swallowed and cast a quick glance at Lila. She was staring openmouthed at Alex Kane.

"Jessica, I decided to take the day off after all. I've been cooped up inside too long," he said with a huge grin. Allison was perched on his hip, her arms clasped tightly around his neck. Turning to Lila, he added, "Hi, how's it going?"

Lila smiled blankly and prodded Jessica with her foot.

"Oh, Alex Kane, this is my friend Lila Fowler. Lila, this is Allison's brother."

"Nice to meet you," Lila said hoarsely.

Alexander hitched Allison up a little higher and gave both girls a self-mocking grin. "I couldn't keep my mind on my work today," he said easily. "I just had to come out and join you."

A ripple of excitement traveled up Jessica's spine. He couldn't concentrate? Could it be because he couldn't get her out of his mind?

"Great! Allison made a sand castle already," Jessica said, babbling slightly. Her cheeks on fire, she pointed to Allison's fort. She couldn't believe he had given up on his work just to see her.

"That great big, gigantic castle! You *made* that, Allie?"

Allison beamed. "Yup!"

"How about you just give me a grand tour,

then," he went on, setting Allison on the ground and taking her hand. She led him off, a blissful smile on her little round face. It was obvious that she adored her big brother.

Jessica and Lila both followed them with their eyes. When they were out of earshot, Lila turned to Jessica with a dazed expression.

"God," she breathed, her eyes wide. "I didn't know musicians had muscles like that."

Jessica shook her head. "Me neither."

"I take it back about you making a big mistake, Jess. I don't blame you one bit."

Silently Jessica shook her head again. As she looked at Alex Kane kneeling in the sand beside Allison, she felt a rush of urgency. She had to get cracking on that stupid recorder. She had to prove to him that she was the perfect match for him!

Seven

" 'The Constitution of the United States is the unique and indispensable foundation of our nation's government, guaranteeing all of us our individual rights and liberties and setting the all-important guidelines for federal and state governments.' *Yech!*"

Elizabeth wrinkled her nose and scribbled out the sentence. "That sounds so pompous," she muttered. Sighing heavily, she rested her head against the back of the lounge chair. Hot afternoon sunlight beat down on her face. *This paper is never going to get written,* she grumbled to herself.

Yawning, Elizabeth stretched her toes and turned her head to look vacantly at the swimming pool. All day she had been sitting on the patio in the backyard, trying to get some work done on her history paper, and she felt tired and bored and uninspired. She glanced at her watch: three-thirty. A whole Saturday almost gone, and with nothing to show for it.

"Hi, Albert," she crooned as the dog padded toward her, dripping wet from a swim. She fondled his ears and gazed into his shining brown eyes, adding, "I just can't concentrate today."

He panted quietly.

"I know," she said with a soft laugh. "I'm just being a wimp." Leaning back again, she squinted up at the brilliant sky. Maybe it was just too bright, she decided. The blinding glare was making her sleepy. Maybe if she wore her sunglasses . . .

Suddenly she realized that when last seen, her sunglasses had been on Jessica's head. *She'd better not have taken them to the beach,* Elizabeth thought grimly. Heaving herself up off the lounge chair, she went inside and climbed the stairs, Prince Albert trailing behind.

In the doorway of Jessica's room Elizabeth paused for a moment. Even assuming her sunglasses were there and not perched on Jessica's nose, there was no telling exactly what pair of shoes they were stuck inside or what pile of laundry they were buried under. With a sigh she meandered around Jessica's room, picking things up and looking underneath. No sunglasses.

But when she lifted her best silk scarf off the bureau, she found Jessica's recorder under it. Elizabeth looked at it for a long minute. Then she looked at the door. Prince Albert was watching her.

With a guilty, self-conscious laugh, she picked up the recorder and sat on the edge of Jessica's bed. "Just for a second," she assured the dog. "I'm just going to try it again."

She played a few experimental notes and held the last one for as long as she could while she kept her eyes fixed blankly on the window. Even though she felt a nagging tingle of guilt, she scanned the room hastily for the recorder book. When she found it, she opened it up to the first lesson again and began following the instructions.

Heaving a rumbling, contented sigh, Prince Albert lay down with his chin on his paws and watched her. Totally absorbed, Elizabeth practiced the recorder, trying new fingerings and gradually learning to read the notes. A patience she never knew she had helped her go over and over the repetitive exercises. When she successfully played a simple rendition of Brahms's *Lullaby*—and it actually sounded *right*—she felt an absurd rush of happiness. She was really making music!

Smiling happily to herself, Elizabeth took a deep breath and repeated the first few measures, concentrating on smooth transitions and a steady tone. She felt a bit light-headed from blowing so much, and her fingertips were becoming slightly sore from pressing down on the holes, but she decided to continue anyway. Eagerly she turned to the next lesson and glanced at her watch.

To her surprise Elizabeth saw she had been playing Jessica's recorder for an hour. And she had promised herself she wasn't even going to touch it! Biting her lip, she gave Prince Albert a guilty look. "Oops. I wasn't supposed to do this, you know. You really should have stopped me."

The dog looked up at her, then put his chin down on his paws again and sighed.

"Well, don't tell anyone, OK?" Elizabeth continued, hiding the recorder once again and brushing her hands on her shorts. "Jess would be pretty angry if she knew I was doing this." She stood at the bureau for a moment, a faraway look in her eyes.

An episode from a few months earlier sprang into her memory. Determined to change her appearance, Jessica had dyed her hair and given herself a new, sophisticated look. She had even managed to see an agent about some fashion modeling. But when Elizabeth went to pick her up at the modeling agency, the owner said he preferred Elizabeth's image to Jessica's. Elizabeth could still see the look of hurt and embarrassment on her twin's face.

And then there was the time when Jessica had taken gourmet cooking lessons and made plans to cook their parents a special anniversary dinner. Not knowing that, Elizabeth gave them tickets to a dinner theater and Jessica's plans were spoiled. There were plenty of instances when Jessica had felt overshadowed or was made to look stupid by something Elizabeth did, even though it was inadvertent on Elizabeth's part.

Not this time, Elizabeth promised her reflection in the mirror. *I'm not going to compete with her and make her feel bad.*

With a pang of regret she touched the recorder, outlined by the thin silk scarf that covered it. She sighed. "Oh, well."

"Hi, Liz. Looking for something?"

Elizabeth whirled around, her cheeks blazing, as Jessica strolled in and tossed her beach bag on the bed. "Oh—uh, I—do you have my sunglasses?" she stammered, remembering her original reason for nosing around in Jessica's room.

"Yeah, sorry," Jessica admitted, giving her twin a disarming smile. "Did you need them?"

Feeling guilty, Elizabeth hastily shook her head. "It doesn't matter." Blushing, she backed through the door to the bathroom that connected their rooms. "Sorry I was poking around."

"It's OK, Liz."

Elizabeth nodded and paused on the threshold.

"Alex came to the beach to pick up Allison," Jessica remarked as she studied her reflection in the full-length mirror. She turned her face to one side to examine her profile and grimaced anxiously. "I guess I'd better get going on that stupid recorder. I told him I'm pretty good at it."

While Elizabeth watched, Jessica began flinging clothes around, searching for the instrument. Elizabeth cleared her throat. "Um, I think it might be on your bureau."

Jessica tossed the scarf aside. "Yup—here it is. Oh, and this is your scarf, too. Boy," she continued, scrambling onto her bed, "I hope I can get good if I practice a lot."

"I know you can," Elizabeth declared, feeling her cheeks flaming scarlet again. "Just practice, Jess. You'll be great."

"You really think so?"

"Sure. Really."

Jessica smiled happily and leaned over to pick the lesson book off the floor. As Elizabeth hurried back to her own bedroom, she heard the beginnings of shrill, impatient piping from Jessica. And she forced herself not to think about how terribly her sister played.

"It looks as if I might be designing a new kitchen for Mrs. Wilson," Alice Wakefield said. She served herself some spinach salad and passed the bowl to Elizabeth. "She's acting as excited as a girl on her first date, too!"

"Maybe we ought to have a new kitchen someday," Jessica suggested hopefully. "Something really wild, maybe."

Mrs. Wakefield gave her a dry look. "Is something wrong with our kitchen?"

"Well . . . not exactly. But it's just that it's been that way *forever*, Mom."

Elizabeth shook her head. If it was up to her, she wouldn't change a thing in the house. When her mother designed something, it was with taste and style that lasted for years. Everything about the house was perfect, in Elizabeth's opinion. And the kitchen was her favorite room—a sunny, inviting room with Spanish tiles and hanging plants.

"Sorry, but I'm afraid it's just staying that way. *Forever*."

"Gee, Jess, I don't know how you can put up with us." Mr. Wakefield grinned and leaned forward to tousle Jessica's hair. "Pass the pepper, please."

Jessica pouted for a few seconds, then she giggled. "Well, it *is* a real burden. Oh, you know what I heard? Bruce told Lila they're having a pledge week for his fraternity pretty soon."

"Now, there's a hot news flash for you, Liz," Mr. Wakefield said.

"Right. Let me stop the presses right now." Elizabeth's eyes twinkled as she looked across the dinner table at her twin. Because Jessica was president of the Pi Beta Alpha sorority, she took all fraternity news seriously. Bruce Patman, the president of the exclusive fraternity, Phi Epsilon, was the richest, most stuck-up boy at school. The license plates on his black Porsche spelled out his motto: 1BRUCE1.

Jessica stuck out her tongue at her twin, raised a forkful of linguini with clam sauce.

"So anyway," Mrs. Wakefield continued, smiling, "I heard you practicing the recorder this afternoon, Jess. You sounded really good."

Jessica put her fork down quickly. "You think so?"

"Yes—and to tell you the truth, I was really surprised," Mrs. Wakefield confessed with a sheepish grin.

"Well, I *have* been practicing. . . ."

"I guess you were getting a little pooped near the end, though. You did hit a few high notes that nearly made my hair stand on end."

Mr. Wakefield choked on his water. "Alice," he gasped, his brown eyes twinkling with shocked laughter. "That's no way to encourage a budding artist."

She shrugged and gave Jessica a loving smile. "Well, you *were* practicing a long time. You must have used up your whole quota of oxygen for the week."

"It didn't *seem* like that long," Jessica said, looking slightly puzzled.

In a flash Elizabeth realized what had happened. Her mother had heard *her* practicing first, and then Jessica, and thought it was Jessica all along. Elizabeth swallowed her food with difficulty. She felt just terrible. Mrs. Wakefield's praise had made Jessica think she was really good. But it didn't take a trained musician to hear that Jessica was really *awful*. In Jessica's hands the recorder sounded like the death agonies of a sacrificial victim.

"You know, you're right," Jessica went on. She bit her lower lip thoughtfully, a speculative gleam in her eyes. Elizabeth knew her twin was thinking about Alex Kane. "I guess I am getting pretty good."

"Maybe you can give us a recital one of these days," their father suggested.

"That's a great idea," Mrs. Wakefield chimed in. "Too bad Liz doesn't play, too—we could have duets."

Elizabeth gave her twin a weak smile. *Now what have I done?* she moaned inwardly.

"You know, Liz. For some reason I always thought you might turn out to be musical," Mr. Wakefield said suddenly. He gave her a smile and put down his napkin. "I guess I was wrong."

"I guess so."

"Well, Liz can't be good at everything," Jessica commented loftily.

"No, I guess not," mumbled Elizabeth. She didn't know what she was going to do now. But at the moment she didn't think telling the truth would go over too well. Jessica would be furious with her, and Elizabeth knew she would deserve it!

Eight

On Monday morning Robin plodded up the wide stone stairs to the main entrance of Sweet Valley High. On each step people sat in the sunshine in groups of two or three, chatting and laughing. She looked at them stormily as she passed, feeling a hot sting of resentment because they all seemed so happy and unconcerned. None of them had to puzzle out the most important decision of *their* lives. Everyone else was just living day to day without driving themselves into a state of panic.

And panic *is definitely the word,* she commented to herself as she pushed through the wide double doors. She might have *told* George she would stay in California, but just saying it didn't solve the problem the way she had thought it would.

She really didn't feel as though she had reached a final decision, especially because her mother had spent the weekend talking about all the wonderful things Aunt Fiona had done for them. Mrs. Wilson had also talked about how important it was to her that Robin get a good education at Sarah Lawrence. And then Robin had started thinking once again about all the New York college had to offer, and she was right back where she started.

There was a stack of school newspapers just inside the door. Robin leaned down to pick up a copy of *The Oracle* and opened it as she walked down the hall.

"Hey, Robin!"

She turned around at the sound of her name. Penny Ayala, editor in chief of the paper, was coming toward her. "Hi, Penny."

"Hi. Did you see the article Liz did about you?"

Raising her eyebrows in surprise, Robin shook her head. The paper rustled in her hands as she riffled through it swiftly.

"Page two," Penny offered. She pushed her hair behind her ears as she waited.

"Oh, about the diving championship," Robin said in a dull tone. She sighed, skimming her eyes over the article. Elizabeth had written about her and Tracy vying for the coveted first-place medal. The article also supplied the date and time for the meet, which meant that a whole contingent of Sweet Valley kids would be there, Robin realized without much enthusiasm.

"I guess I'll have a big audience to see me blow it," she muttered.

Penny gave her a puzzled look. "What are you talking about? It sounds like it's almost a sure thing you'll win."

"Yeah, well—sure things aren't always so sure."

Penny's puzzled look increased, and Robin smiled ruefully. "I'm just in a bad mood. See you later."

"OK, Robin," Penny replied slowly. "Is everything all right?"

Robin opened her mouth to speak, but then she shut it slowly and shook her head. "No, but I'll survive. Thanks."

As Robin turned away, she caught a glimpse of Annie Whitman, standing and talking to some other girls. Their gazes met, and a wave of anger and hurt washed over her. She still couldn't get over the fact that Annie had blabbed her secret to George.

And in a way, Annie seemed to stand for all the things Robin wasn't anymore: carefree, happy, not having to face any important adult decisions. Annie was always so easygoing and lighthearted, taking one day at a time. Robin just couldn't bring herself to face her. The rational side of her knew she was being a little unreasonable, but the hurt, irrational side wanted someone to blame her problems on. Annie was just the person.

Suddenly Annie broke away from her friends and started walking toward Robin, a determined look on her face. But Robin just turned on her heel and strode purposefully in the opposite direction. The last thing she needed right now was more excuses from Annie. And besides, having an argument with her would be the absolute worst way to start a week that was definitely going to get worse—especially since her aunt was arriving on Wednesday evening.

Deep in thought, Jessica hooked her heels over the lowest rung of her stool and bit the side of her thumb. Nothing was going quite right. Across the kitchen island of the Kanes' house, Allison was gazing at her with a silent plea in her big brown eyes. The sound of Alex playing the piano in the sun-room broke the stillness.

"Can't we go play on the beach, Jessica?"

"In a second."

Deep in thought, Jessica pulled on the chain of her gold lavaliere and frowned. There had to be a way to cement the romance between her and Alex. Here it was, a week after she had started baby-sitting, and things hadn't progressed at all. The problem was, Jessica mused, that whenever she was there, he was glued to his piano and his composing. If only she could drag him away from it long enough, she'd be able to dazzle him. . . .

"Could I have some milk? Chocolate milk? Please?" Allison added in an earnest tone when Jessica didn't respond.

Slowly she came down to earth. "OK, sure." Miffed, she jumped off her stool and flounced over to the refrigerator. *It's so frustrating,* she thought as she dragged a full gallon jug of milk from inside.

She stared at the milk for a moment and pictured herself dropping it: milk everywhere, Allison shrieking in alarm. And then Alex would rush in, the light of anxious concern in his gorgeous brown eyes. As he took her in his arms, he would murmur in an emotion-choked voice, "Thank goodness! I thought something terrible had happened to you! I'm just so grateful you're all right! If I had to lose you now . . ."

Then she could laugh—a small, slightly sheepish laugh—and confess to him that the phrase of music she had heard him playing had been so hauntingly moving, so arresting, so soul-stirring, that he had struck an answering chord in the depths of her heart; she had forgotten where she was, who she was . . .

"Jessica?"

She jerked to her senses. *What a lousy idea. I'd just have to clean up all that milk. I'm wearing my best sandals, too.*

Forcing a smile, she mixed a glass of chocolate milk for Allison, but her thoughts honed in on Alex again. The more remote he was, the more she was determined to get him.

"I'll be right back, OK?" She looked Allison squarely in the eyes, adding, "You stay here and drink that nice milk I made you."

The little girl nodded solemnly, a chocolate mustache outlining her upper lip. Then Jessica turned on her heel and hurried into the living room. Through the door to the sun-room she could see Alexander's back as he sat at the piano. Sheets of notation paper were spread in front of him, and every time he played a bar of music, he would jot down the notes with his mechanical pencil.

Her heart quickened, and she smoothed her skirt self-consciously. She waited for him to sense that she was there. He would feel her presence behind him, and he would turn around with her name on his lips. Any minute now. Any minute now he would see her. Any—

"Uh—oh, excuse me," she stammered, flushing pink as he finally turned around.

"Yeah? Oh, hi, Jessica. Need something?"

At least a dozen answers flashed into her mind, but she didn't dare use them. "Well, you see—I was wondering . . ."

She fidgeted with her lavaliere for a moment, trying to think of a good excuse. Every time she looked into his eyes she felt her heart turn somersaults. Her gaze lighted on a stack of sheet music by the piano.

"I was wondering if I could ask you about my recorder music," she said smoothly, moving toward him. Smiling casually, she reached out a hand to riffle through the loose pages.

With a strangled yelp, Alexander sprang off the piano bench. "Don't! Don't touch that!"

She snatched her hand back. "Oops."

"That's the third movement of my symphony," he explained apologetically. "Sorry—I didn't mean to bite your head off." He blinded her with a smile.

"Now, what was that about your music?" he prompted, straightening the pages of notation paper and stealing a quick glance at his watch.

Jessica bit her lip. This wasn't going well at all. Alex seemed too impatient to get back to work. "I was just, you know, looking for something more advanced, more challenging to play."

"Well. Mmm, let me see here." He turned to a pile of music on a shelf and began flipping through the stack. "Here's some Debussy. Do you think you can handle that?"

"Sure," she replied easily. She had no idea what or who Debussy was.

He held out the book with a friendly smile, but his eyes still strayed to his piano and the pages of his score.

"Which is your favorite piece?" Jessica stalled.

Stifling a sigh, Alexander said, "There's a really great étude in here."

"An étude."

They looked at each other for a moment. Alex raised his eyebrows and nodded toward the piano. "Well . . ."

"Well?" Jessica echoed, trying to sound mature and knowing.

He waited for her to go.

With another wistful smile, she took the book of Debussy music and backed away. He still didn't seem to be falling for her. Either that or he was hiding it *very* well. "I'll be in the kitchen with Allison, I guess. Let me know if you need anything."

"OK. Thanks, Jessica."

"Oh, thank *you*." She tried another meaningful glance as she backed up a few more steps. "See you later."

But he turned back to the piano without another word. As Jessica walked back to the kitchen, she decided not to give up on Alex. Getting him to notice her was just going to take a *little* more work than she had planned.

"Come on, Amy! You're supposed to be next to Maria!" Robin scowled at Amy Sutton, a little surprised at how upset she was.

"I thought you said next to Sandy," Amy replied in an injured tone. She faced Robin, hands on her hips, and tossed back her streaky blond hair. "Just make up your mind," she complained.

Robin blushed and looked past Amy to the other cheerleaders. They were all looking at her in a skeptical way. The sun beat down on her, adding to the headache that had been nagging at her all day. Now she remembered. She *had* told Amy to stand next to Sandra Bacon. "Sorry," she mumbled. "You're right."

From the corner of her eye, she saw Amy give Jessica a half-hidden smirk. A wave of embarrassment washed over Robin. *They must think I'm going crazy or something.*

And maybe I am, she added inwardly. Her aunt was due to arrive the next day, Wednesday, and Robin was looking forward to it about as much as she would to a ten-year prison term.

Her aunt was going to expect an unambiguous yes from her, and Robin still wasn't sure she could give one. She felt as though she were being pulled in two, with George on one side, and her mother and aunt on the other.

Suddenly Robin thought she was about to burst into tears in front of everyone. Horrified, she turned away and bent down to retie her sneakers. *I'm totally losing it,* she thought miserably. *I don't know what to do.*

"OK," Jessica called, sending Robin a speculative glance. "Let's run the 'Let's Go' with handstands and cartwheels from both sides."

As Robin stood up, she watched the cheerleading squad run through their standard cheer. Her gaze fell on Annie Whitman, and a pang of loneliness squeezed her heart. If only Robin had someone she could talk to, a friend to turn to. Usually that someone was Annie. But Annie had betrayed her.

"I'm on my own," she whispered. The realization hit her with finality. She had to make a decision and stick to it. She had to get through a computer class test tomorrow with an A. She had to pull herself through the diving championships. All on her own, with no one to turn to.

Shaking her head, she tramped back to join the line. Knowing she was on her own was bad enough. But knowing that whatever she decided someone would be upset and disappointed was even worse. And at this point whatever was best for her didn't even matter. At this point her own happiness didn't count for anything at all.

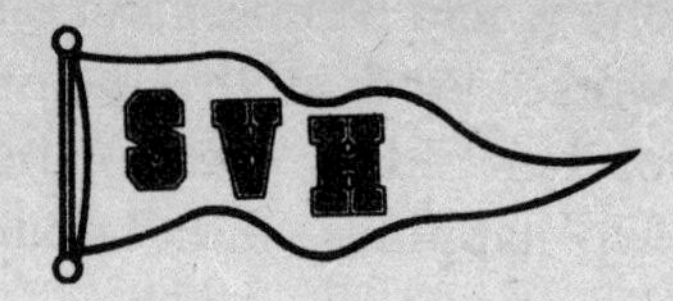

Nine

Jittery with nerves, Robin perched on the arm of the sofa and twisted her fingers together. From the kitchen the sound of her mother clattering dishes together put Robin even more on edge. Any minute now her aunt would arrive. Robin thought she would be sick just thinking about the confrontation. Part of her wanted to put it off for as long as possible, and another part of her just wanted to get it over with—like ripping off a bandage in one sharp movement.

"I'll just tell her I haven't decided yet, that I'm not sure," she whispered under her breath. She bit her lower lip. "There's nothing wrong with that."

At least the boys, Adam and Troy, were out at a late baseball practice. Robin could be glad they were out of the way, anyway, and not rushing around creating their usual chaos.

A car door slammed out in the street. "Mom! She's here," Robin croaked. She jumped to her feet as she spoke and hurried to a front window. Outside, a taxi had pulled up to the curb, and the driver was just opening the trunk. As Robin watched, the back door opened.

Fiona Maxwell, one of New York City's most respected artists, emerged from the backseat of the cab. Tall, gray-haired, and elegantly dressed, she stood on the sidewalk and surveyed the house. Then she turned slowly to appraise the surrounding houses and barked an order to the driver. Robin could see her aunt's lips move as she gestured regally for him to carry her luggage up to the door.

Robin felt herself stiffen with anxiety. Even before her aunt was in the house, the sheer force of her personality was making itself felt. In another moment she would be there, judging them, criticizing every little thing, or else deciding that some detail actually met with her sky-high standards.

"Oh—here she is, and I look terrible," Mrs. Wilson said, patting her short brown hair nervously as she ran in from the kitchen. She tugged on Robin's elbow. "Don't just stand there! Come say hello to your aunt."

Robin forced herself to follow her mother to the front door. As they reached it, there was a loud, impatient knocking sound.

"Well, you decided to let me in, I see," Fiona Maxwell announced as Mrs. Wilson opened the door.

"Oh, Fiona, it's so good to see you! I didn't mean to keep—"

"I know! I'm just teasing you! Well, I must say," she continued, sweeping in through the door, "I always forget what a small town this is. Over here, driver."

The taxi driver, looking harassed and exhausted, lugged her Gucci suitcases in and deposited them in the hallway. But his eyes lit up when Ms. Maxwell tipped him ten dollars. Robin and her mother stood by silently, waiting.

"So . . ." Unwrapping the silk scarf from her throat, Fiona Maxwell turned slowly around in the living room, looking down her nose at every detail. With a critical sniff she fingered the necklace of chunky semiprecious stones she was wearing and gave a firm nod.

"I like what you've done with this room, Irene. I wouldn't have used the same color scheme, given the light you have. And, of course, this cluttered country look is rather dated. But we do have different tastes." She finished with a broad smile, which seemed to suggest that, of course, her taste was superior.

"Can I get you some tea, Fiona?" Mrs. Wilson offered.

"Tea?" she scoffed, rolling her eyes dramatically. With a grand gesture, she declared, "I think a good strong cup of black coffee is more like it. I am absolutely dead after that flight, even though I came first class, as usual. You just don't find the same quality of service anymore."

"I'll be right back, then. Robin, why don't you tell Aunt Fiona all your news," Mrs. Wilson prodded before hurrying off.

Ms. Maxwell settled herself in the middle of the sofa and looked around again. Finally her eyes came to rest on Robin.

"You're certainly looking good these days, dear. I'm relieved to see you finally managed to dispose of that baby fat you carried around with you for so long."

A fiery blush swept across Robin's cheeks. There was no way to accept such a backhanded compliment. But that was just the way her aunt was.

"And what's this I hear about your diving?" she continued. "Honestly, Robin. I had no idea you aspired to be an *athlete,* of all things."

"I really like it, Aunt Fiona. It's—it's fun."

Robin felt ashamed of the weakness in her voice. But her aunt's personality was so forceful that it left her feeling drained.

Fiona Maxwell sniffed. "Fun! There must be better ways to amuse yourself. At Sarah Lawrence you'll certainly want to immerse yourself in cultural events, lectures, concerts, and all the other intellectual offerings."

Now! Do it now! Robin urged herself silently. She drew a deep breath.

"And listen, Robin. You know how I am," her aunt continued in a softer tone, her brown eyes flashing with enthusiasm. "Don't think I'm not thrilled, absolutely thrilled, that you've been accepted by my old alma mater. It means a great deal to me to know you're going."

"Me, too," Mrs. Wilson chimed in as she returned. She set a cup of coffee down in front of her sister and shot Robin a warning glance. "Robin is so grateful—"

"Grateful, schmateful!" Ms. Maxwell interrupted with a dismissive wave. "She's a smart girl, and she deserves my help. I wouldn't have it any other way."

Robin swallowed hard over a lump in her throat. She felt completely paralyzed. She knew she had to say something soon, but she couldn't make her mind work. All she could think of was how true her aunt's words were. She *wouldn't* have it any other way. It was Sarah Lawrence or nothing. If only her aunt weren't so opinionated, so concerned with running people's lives!

Stretching luxuriously, Ms. Maxwell looked around the living room again. Then she bent toward the coffee table and picked up a paperback book by one corner. She held it away from her as though it were a smelly piece of garbage. "Really, Irene. This is such trash. I read the first four paragraphs and threw it right away."

"Oh, my neighbor, Evelyn King, gave it to me. She told me it was so good."

"If she's the woman in the house next door," Aunt Fiona said in a tone of withering scorn, "I'm not surprised. I noticed they've put up one of those dreary carriage boy statues since the last time I was here. If there is anything more dreadfully tacky, I'm sure I don't know what it is."

"Oh—I suppose you have a point there," Mrs. Wilson agreed. There was a hint of embarrassed apology in her voice as she looked at her older sister.

Robin felt a spark of indignation. Who cared if the Kings had a tacky statue? And why did her mother have to make excuses? Already Robin could feel a wave of resentment building up against her aunt, on top of the panic and confusion!

"Take my advice, Irene, and don't take *her* advice on reading material. Obviously the woman has an extraordinarily boring and uninspired mind."

"Well, if you say so, Fiona." Mrs. Wilson smoothed her skirt down nervously. "You know, we're so interested in your new show in L.A. I guess you must have gotten all the talented genes in the family, because I know I sure don't have an artistic bone in my body."

"Well, talent is a gift, that's true. Of course, it takes hard work and dedication, too. But this is just a small gallery," Ms. Maxwell said with a shrug. "I'm really doing them a favor by showing there. Anyway, when I get back, I want to take you all out to that lovely little place we ate in once before."

"The Cote d'Or?" Robin suggested doubtfully. The Cote d'Or in nearby Malvina was one of the most glamorous, expensive restaurants in the area. It wasn't what she would call just "a lovely little place."

"That's the one. A little celebration dinner in honor of Robin carrying on the family tradition."

Robin met her mother's pointed look and felt herself flush. If she was going to mention that there was some doubt about her carrying on the family tradition, now was the time. But she couldn't get the words out. In her mind she could see her aunt's outraged expression, hear the outburst of anger.

"Now tell me all about the new kitchen you're planning, Irene. I hope you aren't thinking of designing it yourself."

The opportunity was lost. By not saying anything, Robin had consented to her aunt's plans. And now the deal was settled. Talking about the new kitchen, the payoff, was proof of that.

I've been traded for a new kitchen, Robin thought in amazement. But she still couldn't speak. Her aunt was holding court like a monarch. Interrupting now would be a major crime.

"Well, I've been talking to a designer in town," Mrs. Wilson admitted.

"*Please!* Not a housewife who took a correspondence course in interior decorating, I hope!"

"No—she's a professional. She's really very good. She's the mother of some girls in Robin's class," Mrs. Wilson stammered on awkwardly. "And, well, we've come up with some fabulous ideas. . . ."

Ms. Maxwell raised her eyebrows, obviously impatient with the chatter. She liked to talk herself but was too opinionated to listen to anyone else.

"In fact, I have a few sketches she's made

just as a rough idea," Robin's mother went on. "I'll go get them."

As she hurried from the room, Robin felt herself wondering why it was they had to treat Aunt Fiona as though she were the Queen of England. She was part of the family, but they couldn't be relaxed and comfortable with her. Robin suspected the reason her aunt didn't encourage warmth from them was because she liked to keep them off-balance.

That conclusion made her decide she had to say something. She had to demonstrate that she wasn't completely unable to function without her aunt's support.

Robin cleared her throat. "Uh, I thought you might want to know—I'm going to be in a big diving championship this Sunday, Aunt Fiona. My coach thinks I have a good shot at winning."

"Oh, Robin. I'm sure that's very nice for someone else who doesn't have your opportunities. But really, don't you think it's time for you to move ahead? This diving sounds like a waste of your time and energy," her aunt declared.

"But—" Robin licked her lips. "It's really important to me," she said. She knew she had to stand up to her aunt about *something*, or she would just crumble completely.

But her aunt's mouth was set in a stern, uncompromising line. "Well, you won't be able to pursue it in New York, that I can tell you. I'm not sending you to an expensive private college so you can spend your time swimming."

"Diving," Robin said, gritting her teeth.

"Whatever. Oh, for goodness' sake, go ahead and go to your little competition, Robin. But don't expect me to sit on some hard bleachers in a crowd of screeching mothers to watch you."

"No, I don't expect you to," Robin agreed softly. She kept her eyes on the floor.

"Be sensible, Robin," her aunt continued. "I can understand your having some schoolgirl hobbies, but you're about to go off to college next year. You have responsibilities, you know."

Robin nodded mutely as her throat grew tight.

Her aunt sighed. "Ah, what a treat to be young again and off to Sarah Lawrence for the first time! Such an adventure, such joy in learning and being and creating! It's a crime to waste such a precious time on trivial matters, Robin. Believe me, I *know* what I'm talking about."

As her aunt's words swept over her, dragging her along like a swift current, Robin wondered to herself whether she was ready for college even if she did want to go. Growing up suddenly—that's what it would be. Or at least that was what her aunt was saying. It all sounded so serious and urgent. Robin was looking forward to college—the classes, studying, stretching her mind—but she also enjoyed being a cheerleader, and she loved her diving. . . .

"Here they are! The boys put a whole load of dirty laundry on top of them, so that's why it took me so long to find them." Breathless, Mrs. Wilson trotted back into the living room carrying several sheets of drawing paper in her hand. As she settled herself next to her sister on the couch, she gave Robin a happy smile. "You don't know how happy I am about this, Fiona. It's just like a dream come true."

More like a nightmare, Robin said to herself. Fighting back tears, she jumped up from her chair and walked hastily from the room.

"Here you go. A large root beer," Enid Rollins said, sliding into the booth across from Elizabeth.

"Thanks." Elizabeth took the drink from her best friend and smiled.

Over the rim of her paper cup, she cast a glance around. Going to the Dairi Burger after school was a Sweet Valley High tradition, and the place was packed on that Thursday. At one table The Droids, Sweet Valley's own student rock group, were hunched over some sheet music. Drummer Emily Mayer was rapping out a beat on the tabletop with her sticks while the others nodded. And near the jukebox a loud burst of laughter erupted from a group of boys as Winston Egbert demonstrated a chicken dance.

Enid twirled her soda straw around and cupped her chin in one hand. "One more day of school, then the weekend. I can't wait until Friday!"

"I know what you mean," Elizabeth agreed. "This week is taking forever."

She turned her gaze toward the door just in time to see Jessica coming in with Amy and Cara. "Look out," she said lightly. "Here comes the hurricane."

Jessica caught sight of her at the same instant and bounced over. "Hi! I'm dying of thirst! Can I have a sip?" she asked as she reached for Elizabeth's root beer. She tipped it up and gulped half the soda before Elizabeth could rescue it.

"Thanks," Jessica said breathlessly. "Cheerleading was a total disaster scene today. I swear, Robin was acting like the world was about to explode into a hundred and thirty-seven million pieces. She kept messing up, screaming at Annie—"

"Annie?" Enid cut in, her green eyes wide with surprise. "But aren't she and Robin really good friends?"

"*Were* good friends," Jessica corrected. She hitched her pink duffel bag over one shoulder and shrugged. "But Robin got this bizarre idea that Annie told George on purpose about Robin getting accepted at college so he'd be all mad and Annie could snap him up. Ridiculous, huh?"

As her twin spoke, a flush of guilt rippled through Elizabeth. She knew that she was the one who had blurted Robin's secret to George. Now Annie was suffering for it.

Cara and Amy were gesturing impatiently for Jessica from another table, and Jessica suddenly looked chagrined. She hadn't meant to tell Elizabeth. "Listen, don't tell anyone I told you that, OK? I shouldn't have said anything. See you later." She raced away again.

"Liz, what' wrong?" Enid asked, concerned.

Elizabeth looked up slowly, a blush coloring her cheeks. "Robin's arguing with Annie—that's my fault. I saw George and told him. I didn't realize this would happen."

"Well, you could just tell Robin, then, couldn't you?" Enid suggested in a level tone. She pushed her straw into the crushed ice in her cup.

Elizabeth suddenly felt even worse. They were discussing Enid's ex-boyfriend, after all. "Yeah." She sighed. "I was going to apologize last week, but I sort of forgot."

"Oh, no. That's a capital crime, Elizabeth Wakefield!" Enid teased gently.

Elizabeth rested her chin in one hand and

sighed. "I don't know—I've been working on this history report and writing an article for the paper." She shook her head. "I've been so busy, it just slipped my mind. And then I've also been sneaking around the house, thinking Jess is going to find out any minute that I'm playing her recorder. Talk about a guilty conscience!" She grinned sheepishly.

Enid gave her a puzzled frown. "Recorder?"

Elizabeth darted a quick look across the Dairi Burger to her twin. Jessica was leaning close to Amy and whispering urgently in her ear. Turning back to Enid, she explained, "See, Jess bought a recorder to impress this music student whose sister she baby-sits for, and I started playing it. I'm not sure what to do."

"I guess I must be missing something," Enid said. "I don't get what the big problem is."

"It's just that I promised myself I wasn't going to butt in on the things Jess wanted to do. But I just tried it out, and I really like it, Enid. I think I could be good at it." Her blue-green eyes sparkled with enthusiasm.

"Sounds like you're pretty serious."

"I am. I don't know—maybe I realized a while ago that I needed something else besides writing. I think the recorder could be it," she finished wistfully. "But I *can't*."

Enid glanced across the room at Jessica. With

a wry twist to her mouth she said, "You know, it's hard to believe she's really all that interested—if it's just to impress some guy. Why don't you just ask her if she cares?"

"I know." Elizabeth shook her head. "But I can't. She'll just think I'm trying to squeeze her out or outshine her. I don't want her to feel like that's what I'm doing."

"But that's *not* what you're doing, Liz."

Elizabeth shrugged helplessly.

"Well, I don't know what to tell you, then." Enid sighed.

Staring down into her empty cup, Elizabeth just shook her head slowly. "Me neither. I don't know what to do."

Ten

Jessica pushed her heels into the hot sand and let her breath out slowly. It was Saturday afternoon, and she still wasn't making any headway with Alex Kane. She was beginning to wonder if he was totally immune to her. It was hard to believe, but that's how it seemed.

"What's this word?" Allison crawled over to Jessica and shoved a picture book in her lap. One little finger pointed to the page.

"That's a long one. Grasshopper," Jessica muttered. Even as she spoke, she turned her gaze back to the bungalow on top of the dunes. Sunlight twinkled on the windows.

"Can I ask Alex to come play with us?" Allison asked. She flipped through her picture book in a bored way. "I want Alex."

"Alex is working, remember? Mommy and Daddy are in San Francisco again, and we're not supposed to bother Alex while he's composing. If you need something, that's why I'm here."

Allison stuck out her lower lip and trickled sand through her fingers. Watching her, Jessica decided she knew just how Allison felt! There was nothing more infuriating than being told not to talk to the one person you were interested in. But despite the way things were going —or not going—Jessica was still interested in Alex. It was just an exceptional challenge.

And, she reminded herself sensibly, she had been very good so far about not disturbing him while he was working. It couldn't hurt if she just went in and stopped by the sun-room for a little chat, could it? Just to say hello, ask politely how the symphony was going? Maybe point out that he did have her phone number, after all?

"How about practicing your recorder?" Jessica suggested to Allison. She narrowed her eyes speculatively at the house.

"OK. I'll go—"

"No, no. You wait here, and I'll get it. Don't go away from this spot, though. I'll be right back." Jessica jumped to her feet and trudged through the sand to the beach bungalow. She had made certain "arrangements" when she arrived. It was time to put her plan into action.

She slipped in the back door and scraped the sand from her bare feet. She could hear Alex playing along with a passage of music he had taped on the stereo. Quietly she tiptoed to the sun-room.

Alex was sitting at the piano, a rapt look on his handsome features. His graceful, sensitive hands were poised above the keys.

Jessica cleared her throat loudly.

"Oh—Jessica?" He frowned slightly as he turned his attention away from the music.

Jessica sidled into the room and gave Alex an apologetic smile. "I'm really sorry for disturbing you, but I can't find Allison's recorder. She says it's in here."

Reluctantly he stood up and looked around. "Hmm . . . she did have it in here this morning."

"Maybe she hid it? You know how little kids can be." Under cover of looking for Allison's recorder, Jessica maneuvered herself right next to Alex and followed him closely around the room. She tried to keep him from looking in the bookcase.

"Oops!" She bumped into him deliberately and gave him a melting look. "Excuse me," she said in a low, throaty voice.

He smiled absently and pulled a cushion from

the easy chair. He was so close she could smell the shampoo he used. A ripple of anticipation ran up her spine.

"Maybe"—she turned so she was facing him again and gazed up into his face—"maybe . . ."

Sighing impatiently he moved past her to the overflowing bookcase. Jessica felt a scream of irritation building up inside.

"Hey—here it is," he said, visibly relieved as he pulled the recorder from between two books. He smiled as he handed it to her, then went back to the piano.

Silently Jessica cursed herself for not hiding it in a more difficult place. She had counted on it taking at least fifteen minutes to find. She still hovered nearby.

"Was there something else you needed?"

"Oh, no. I'm going now." She waved the recorder and backed out the door. If she had felt more confident about her own playing, she might have offered to give him a short, private recital. But she had to admit that, at this point, it would probably do more harm that good. She couldn't honestly say that she had made any progress whatever with the instrument. All those stupid exercises were so boring, she usually gave up practicing after five or ten minutes.

Jessica plodded through the sand back to Allison. "Here you go," she said, handing Allison the recorder.

Jessica threw herself back down on their big beach blanket, then rolled over onto her elbows and scowled up at the cottage.

I don't think I'm going to get him with my recorder playing, she confessed to herself. Allison was trilling a quick, complicated melody as though it were as easy as breathing. *There's got to be another way.*

She sat up. "Allison?"

The little girl popped the recorder out of her mouth. "Yup?"

"What does your brother like besides music? Sports?" she suggested hopefully.

Allison wrinkled her nose. "Is that like football? I don't think so."

"Hmm." Frowning at the house again, Jessica said, "How about traveling to exotic places?"

"What's 'zotic places?"

Jessica grimaced. "Forget it." What was it going to *take*? She scowled ferociously at the breaking surf. She was only supposed to stay until five-thirty—just another half hour. She had to make *some* progress before she left for the day. She couldn't accept total failure.

"Can I go ask Alex something?" Allison said timidly.

Jessica shook her head. "You know the rules. Don't disturb him while he's working."

She slumped over, deep in thought. As a last resort she could use the fainting trick. It had gotten her out of tight spots before. Maybe she could use it to get her *into* one. But it was a last-resort measure, because it was a pretty difficult one to use. If it worked, though, she could always stage a miraculous recovery. With brightening hope she decided to go for it. Once more she instructed Allison not to move and went back inside the house.

Alex looked so handsome the way he clenched his jaw, Jessica thought as she stood on the threshold of the room again. Too bad he also looked very irritated.

"What is it *now*, Jessica?"

She raised one hand to her forehead and fluttered her eyelids. "Oh, I just feel so—so—"

Alex stood motionless, staring at her in perplexed surprise.

Staggering slightly, Jessica took a few steps toward him, giving him the perfect chance to catch her as she fell. With a faint moan, she crumpled in a heap on the floor.

"Jessica!" Alex exclaimed. "My god, what's wrong?" He hadn't caught her, but he did kneel beside her and take her hand. And there was a true note of concern in his voice now.

"Oh—did I faint?" Jessica said after pretending to gradually regain consciousness. "I'm so sorry. I didn't want—I mean," she gasped, giving the performance everything she had, "I didn't want anyone to know I was so—"

"What? Are you sick, Jessica? Should I call your mother?"

She gritted her teeth at that but forced a brave smile. "No—that's OK. If you could just help me to the couch, I'll rest. . . ."

"Of course," Alex said warmly.

"I'll be just fine."

She resisted a triumphant smile as he put his strong, warm arms around her. Relaxing all her muscles, she leaned against him as he tried to lift her up off the floor. His face was only inches from hers.

After a long pause, Alex said, "Jessica?"

Tipping back her head, she closed her eyes. "Yes?" she said breathily.

Alex carried her gently to the couch and set her down. "I know I've been a little rude—I get that way when I work—but you seem like such a nice girl, and I couldn't help wondering . . ."

Her voice was a throaty whisper. "Yes?" *Hurry up!* she told him silently.

"Well, I'm going to be leaving at the end of the semester for New York to study at Juilliard, and—"

She flicked her eyes open. *"New York?"*

"Yes, and I was thinking, I'm so busy now—you see, I have to devote all my time to my music—but maybe in a year or two, when I come back . . ."

Not a chance! she retorted silently. *No long-distance relationships for me! Especially one where I take second place to a piano! I don't care how gorgeous you are!*

She glanced casually at her watch. "Oh, look at the time! It's five-thirty, time for me to go. I'm feeling much better now, and I have a date tonight—with my boyfriend," she added quickly, hoping to squelch any hopes Alex had for their getting together. "Sorry I can't stay any longer. And good luck with your symphony. Bye." With a glittering smile, she hopped off the couch and went outside to wave goodbye to Allison. Then, without another look at Alex, she headed for the door.

In spite of his irresistible good looks, Alex Kane had turned out to be one for the reject pile! No sooner had he noticed her than he was setting them up for a long-distance relationship two years in the future! And getting committed to a serious relationship was the one thing Jessica didn't have in mind!

"No, thanks," she muttered as she hopped in the car. "I'm not waiting for *anybody*!"

As Jessica zoomed past a good-looking boy

on a bicycle, she flashed a smile and waved. She didn't give another thought to Alex Kane.

Elizabeth straightened her stiff back and took a deep breath. The particular recorder passage she was working on had tricky fingering, and she kept stumbling over the notes. Part of the reason for her mistakes was that she felt so guilty. Over and over she had told herself she wasn't going to touch Jessica's recorder again. But she just couldn't help it. It was in her system now.

"I've got to say something to her," she muttered as she repositioned her fingers over the holes. "This is getting ridiculous."

The simplified Bach prelude was so beautiful that she hated playing it poorly. She made herself repeat and repeat and repeat it until she had it right.

"Hi, Liz." Jessica strolled into Elizabeth's room and threw herself on the bed. "Hey—you're playing my recorder!"

Elizabeth froze. All the color drained from her face as she stared at her twin. She wished she could disappear.

"I only wanted to try it," she babbled, hastily putting the recorder down. "I wasn't really doing anything. I won't take it again, I promise."

"Go ahead," Jessica said. "I don't care."

"What?" Stunned, Elizabeth looked at her twin. Jessica was flipping through the pages of a magazine by the bed.

Jessica tossed the magazine aside. "I said, I don't care. You can have it if you want."

A laugh of pure relief bubbled up inside Elizabeth. She shook her head, trying to make sense of it all. All that crazy worrying for nothing!

"But—but what about your plan? What about the music student?"

"Well. . . ." Jessica traced circles on the bedspread with one finger. Finally she looked up with a sheepish grin and a twinkle in her blue-green eyes. "Would you believe he's actually one of those guys with *no* time for romance?"

"Come on!"

Jessica giggled. "Yeah. 'I have to devote all my time to my music,' " she quoted dramatically. "Besides, he's going off to New York."

"Oh, Jess," Elizabeth said with a sympathetic laugh. "All that work for nothing!"

"Yeah. What a waste. But go ahead. Let me hear you play."

A fresh wave of guilt passed over Elizabeth as she began to play. She was almost embarrassed to let Jessica know how far she had advanced. "I'm not really that good, you know," she said once she had finished the prelude.

Her twin gave her a steady look. "Right, Liz.

You're just a hundred and thirty-seven times better than I am."

There was an awkward moment. Elizabeth was afraid her prediction would come true, that Jessica would feel hurt and pushed aside. But then Jessica smiled.

"Anyway"—heaving a sigh, Jessica pushed herself up off the bed—"I may not last too much longer on this job. It's cutting into my social life in a big way." She paused by Elizabeth's mirror and gave herself a smile. "And that's *definitely* something to avoid."

Elizabeth chuckled as Jessica breezed through the bathroom doorway and disappeared. It didn't look as if Jessica would bear any deep scars from her thwarted romance, Elizabeth observed. And she didn't seem to have any regrets about giving up the recorder, either.

Now I can play as much as I want! Elizabeth realized, grinning with pure delight.

But as Elizabeth picked up the recorder again, the one subject that had been crowded out for the past few days came back into her mind: Robin and Annie.

I should really do something about that, she decided.

She took her phone book out of a drawer and looked up Robin's number, then picked up the phone receiver. "I hope they aren't eating dinner right now," she muttered as she punched the buttons. It was after six o'clock already. She waited impatiently, listening to the ringing signal. After seven rings, Elizabeth put down the receiver.

Well, it probably isn't that urgent, she said to herself thoughtfully. She didn't feel very convinced, though.

Eleven

"Boys, would you please try to behave yourselves? Honestly!" Mrs. Wilson's voice was edged with irritation as she pulled into the floodlit parking lot of the Cote d'Or.

"Aw, Mom," Troy said, snickering. He batted at Adam's head. "We're not doing anything."

"Well, you'd better not act up in the restaurant! It's very fancy!"

Next to her mother in the front seat, Robin sat with her hands clasped tightly in her lap. The thought of going into the elegant restaurant and eating a lot of rich food made her feel slightly sick. She knew she had to say something that night. She had to put the brakes on somehow, or else things wouldn't slow down again until she found herself in a dormitory room at Sarah Lawrence college.

Troy and Adam poked each other in the ribs one last time and scrambled out of the car. "Can I have a Coke with dinner, Mom?" Adam pleaded.

"Me, too!"

Mrs. Wilson patted nervously at her hair and locked the car door. "Yes, but just one. And don't pester Aunt Fiona about dessert. If she orders one, you can, too."

Robin sat glued to her seat while the rest of her family piled out into the parking lot. Numb, she stared at her hands.

"Robin? Come on! What are you waiting for? We're late already."

No one knows how I feel, she told herself angrily. *No one even realizes how upset I am.*

With a shaky breath, she opened her door and stepped out of the car. The next hour was going to be the hardest of her life. She was sure of that. Like a sleepwalker, she followed her mother and brothers into the expensive French restaurant.

"Yes—Maxwell. Your party is here," the maître d' said, bowing them into the dining room. "This way."

Up ahead, Robin could see her aunt already seated at a table, her chin raised arrogantly as she watched them approach. She looked as though she owned the restaurant, Robin thought as she dropped her gaze. She felt as if she were walking toward her own execution.

"You're ten minutes late, but I'm in a forgiving mood," Fiona Maxwell announced, her tone softening her words a bit. There was a general shuffle as the Wilsons sat down, picked up napkins, and scooted chairs in. "This *is* a night to celebrate, after all."

"How did everything go in L.A., Fiona? Were there a lot of people at the opening?" Mrs. Wilson asked, smiling.

"Another major critical hit, Irene. Beverly Hills fancies itself a real paradise of culture. And the art press was there in full force, all of them drooling, believe me."

"Did anybody buy a painting, Aunt Fiona?" Troy asked. "Everybody in Beverly Hills is a millionaire."

"Troy!" his mother exclaimed. She frowned at him. "Don't be impolite."

"Well, actually, not everybody in Beverly Hills is a millionaire," Ms. Maxwell went on with a tolerant smile. "But they want everyone to think so, so they buy anyway. Three of the large canvases went within the first fifteen minutes!" She had a satisfied look on her face as she rearranged her huge red silk scarf around her shoulders.

Robin did a quick calculation in her head and felt slightly dizzy. She knew what her aunt's large paintings went for. Each one was worth the equivalent of almost a full four years of college!

"That's wonderful!" Mrs. Wilson gasped. "Oh, you must be so excited!"

Aunt Fiona shrugged modestly and opened up her menu. "I'm used to it by now, to tell you the truth. But I can still remember the first painting I sold! Oh, I was just giddy!" She laughed, thinking back to her first triumph. Obviously she was in a good mood.

A waiter appeared suddenly at their table. "May I take your order?" he asked.

Fiona Maxwell held up one hand for silence. "I'm going to order for all of us," she declared in her typically grand and overbearing way. She sent the boys a knowing smile. "Trust me, I won't stick you with something inedible. I think first an endive salad, then pâté de foie gras, and filet mignon. And Cokes for the gentlemen," she added smoothly when Adam and Troy sent their mother agonized glances.

"Merci," the waiter said. He bowed and glided away.

"That all sounds just lovely," Mrs. Wilson said, breathing a happy sigh. She leaned toward Robin and patted her hand. "You're awfully quiet, dear."

Robin felt herself blushing, and she made a small jerking movement with her shoulders. "I—uh—"

"I propose a toast," her aunt cut in. She raised her glass of water and nodded to the others to do the same.

A wave of sickening anxiety built up inside Robin. She reached one hand toward her water and grasped the glass so hard her fingertips turned white. She couldn't look up.

"I propose a toast to my success, and to Robin's. I know she's going to take Sarah Lawrence by storm and do great, significant things."

"All right!" Troy put in, giggling.

There was an expectant pause, and Robin fought down the panic that threatened to overpower her. *They're all waiting for me to say something!* she realized suddenly.

Robin set her glass down on the table. Something inside her rebelled at last: she couldn't let herself be railroaded into someone else's plan for her. She might eventually decide to go to Sarah Lawrence, but no one would make that decision but her. And she couldn't let her concern for other people's feelings cripple her any longer. Everyone would end up hurt that way.

She looked her aunt right in the eye, her chin up. "Aunt Fiona, I'm sorry, but I haven't decided for sure yet whether I can accept your offer."

A horrified silence gripped everyone at the table. Robin could hear her heart pounding in her ears, but she didn't look away from her aunt's wide, outraged eyes.

"Oh, Robin," her mother said finally.

"Is this supposed to be a joke, Robin?" her aunt asked in an icy tone. "Because if it is, I think it's in very poor taste."

Robin shook her head slowly. She couldn't back down now. She knew her whole future was on the line. "No—I-I realize how important it is to you, but it's important to me, too—where I go to school, I mean." She broke off and swallowed hard. "I just—I'm not completely sure if Sarah Lawrence is the right place for me."

Her aunt stared at her frostily. "You mean to tell me, young lady, that you're throwing this opportunity in my face? Is *that* it?"

Mrs. Wilson let out a muffled groan. "No—that's not what she means! Is it, Robin? She is going to Sarah Lawrence, Fiona. She is."

"No!" Robin shook her head desperately. Frightened tears stung her eyes as she continued. "I'm not sure I'm ready to go yet. I'm not sure I want to leave California at all!"

Breathing hard, Fiona Maxwell carefully folded her napkin and set it beside her plate. She was clearly preparing to do battle.

"Whoa, Robin, you better—"

"Adam, keep out of this!" Mrs. Wilson snapped.

Robin closed her eyes briefly. Why couldn't she make anyone understand what she was trying to say?

"Robin," Ms. Maxwell began, her voice deadly calm, "I find it very hard to believe you are in a position to take this attitude. I am prepared to pay your full tuition—"

"But only at Sarah Lawrence?" Robin choked.

"It's an *excellent* school, Robin!" Mrs. Wilson put in quickly. Her voice held a note of panic.

"I think I have a right to decide how and where my money should be spent," Ms. Maxwell went on, completely ignoring her sister. She held Robin's gaze steadily, trying to subdue her.

"Don't I have a right to decide where I go to college?" Robin whispered, trying to remain strong.

At that moment their salads arrived, throwing everyone into confusion. Robin pressed her hands over her mouth and looked down at her plate, her appetite completely gone.

"Thank you; that will do," Ms. Maxwell said, waving the waiter away haughtily. "Robin, I certainly hope this is just last-minute cold feet. You're overexcited, naturally. It's perfectly understandable."

Robin gritted her teeth. "I'm not overexcited. I'm trying to be very *reasonable,* Aunt Fiona—"

"Reasonable?" her aunt scoffed. "Ha!"

"I just need some more time to make up my mind," Robin went on, holding back tears.

"You decide not to go to Sarah Lawrence and you'll never see another penny from me, young lady."

Robin and her aunt stared at each other. No one else in the crowded restaurant mattered to Robin, not her mother, not her brothers. It was just Robin and her aunt. The tension around the table was electric.

Robin broke it with a half sob. "I wouldn't take your money if I were starving to death," she choked out finally. Her mother gasped as she pushed her chair back abruptly and stumbled to her feet.

"Robin!" Fiona Maxwell's voice was hard with indignation.

"No!" Robin cried. Searing tears streamed down her face as she whirled around and raced away. She had to get away from them—all of them. She had never felt so alone in her whole life.

* * *

The only thing Robin could think of was George. All she wanted was to lean against his shoulder and cry her eyes out. She stopped walking—she was hurrying blindly down the sidewalk—and entered a phone booth.

With shaking hands she fumbled in her purse for a coin. She inserted it into the slot and punched in George's phone number.

"G-George!" she sobbed, once he had answered the phone. She wiped tears from her face with the back of her hand.

"What? Robin, what's wrong? You sound so upset."

Instead of answering, she hiccuped on a fresh burst of tears.

"Robin, stop crying and tell me what's wrong. Where are you?" he added, a note of alarm creeping into his voice. "I hear cars."

She looked around herself blankly. "I'm—I'm on Malvina at Broadway and the Coast Road. In front of a hardware store. Could you come get me?" she wailed.

"I'll be right there."

When Robin hung up, she felt slightly better. Hugging her arms around herself, she waited in front of the hardware store. She paced back and forth mechanically, trying to block the scene in the restaurant from her mind. She didn't want to think about it at all.

Twenty minutes later George's car pulled in front of the store. Sighing with relief, she ran to open the door.

"Oh, George," she whimpered as she buried her face in his chest.

"Shh . . . OK, Robin. It's OK." George stroked her hair gently, his lips against her head. "What happened? What are you doing out here?"

Sniffing and catching her breath on sobs, Robin replayed the entire scene at the restaurant for him. She tried to keep her voice calm, but the stifling sense of panic and unfairness gripped her again as she spoke. "And now I don't know what to do!" she concluded, her chin trembling. "Why won't they let me make up my own mind?"

George's face was grim. "They've no right to mess with our plans, Robin. You're staying right here. They can't send you three thousand miles away like you're their property."

Our plans. A chill traveled up Robin's spine. George was doing the same thing her aunt and her mother were doing—deciding what was right for her without asking her what she thought! Robin sat up abruptly. "Can you just take me home?" she asked in a low voice.

"Sure. No problem."

The whole ride passed in dismal silence on Robin's part. She should have known better, she scolded herself. George wasn't going to be impartial and objective about this. He wanted her to stay in California.

But as she sat staring out the window, George kept up an indignant running tirade. He accused everyone but himself of trying to run Robin's life for her. Finally he stopped speaking as he pulled the car up in front of the Wilsons' house.

"Don't—you don't have to come in, OK?"

George smiled, his eyes full of love and concern. "I don't mind, Robin. You know I wouldn't leave you all alone."

But she shook her head vehemently, not trusting herself to meet his eyes. "No, that's not it. I really want to be alone for a while," she told him. Before he could protest, she jumped out of the car and hurried to the front door.

"Why won't people let me decide for myself?" she whispered as she shut the door behind her. A tear slipped down her cheek. "They all say I'm so smart, but they don't think I can make a decision like this myself!"

Just as she was about to drag herself up to her room, the phone rang. For a moment she considered not answering it. But then she thought it might be her mother, calling to see if she was home. She went into the kitchen and picked up the receiver.

"Hello?"

"Robin? Is that you? It's Liz."

Robin closed her eyes briefly. She didn't feel like talking to anyone, even Elizabeth Wakefield. "Hi, Liz. I'm sorry, but I— "

"I just wanted to tell you," Elizabeth cut in anxiously. "I was the one who told George about your getting into Sarah Lawrence. I didn't realize he didn't know. I'm sorry if it was a problem."

It was Liz. Robin stared at the kitchen floor in shock.

"And I heard you were blaming Annie for it, too. I'm really sorry I blabbed, Robin. I hope it wasn't too serious."

Robin let her breath out slowly in a long sigh. "Oh, it doesn't matter anymore," she said, her voice tired and flat.

There was a pause. "Are you all right?" Elizabeth asked with obvious concern. "You sound kind of down."

"I *am* a little down, Liz," Robin replied on a short, bitter laugh.

"Is there anything I can do? I'm coming to your diving finals tomorrow to cheer you on, you know," Elizabeth said in a cajoling tone.

"Diving." Robin shook her head. The diving championship was *tomorrow.* With everything else, she had completely forgotten. She gulped. "Oh, no."

"You'll do fine, Robin. I know you will."

"Thanks, Liz." Robin sighed. She put one hand on her forehead and pushed her hair away from her temples. Her head was throbbing, and she thought she might cry again. "Thanks, Liz," she repeated. "I'll see you tomorrow."

"Good luck," Elizabeth said softly.

As Robin hung up the phone she whispered, "I'm really going to need it!"

Twelve

The sun blazed out of a cloudless sky, and a warm breeze stirred up ripples in the huge swimming pool. Everywhere George looked, people were crowding into lawn chairs and up onto the one set of bleachers overlooking the Sweet Valley Community Pool. The cement around the pool was dark and wet with puddles splashed up from the morning's swim team practice, and there was a faint scent of chlorine in the air.

"The first round of the regional diving championships will begin in fifteen minutes," boomed a voice over the P.A. system. "Fifteen minutes."

A few yards from where George stood, a crowd of giggling girls passed in a cluster. He recognized Jessica Wakefield and Annie Whitman and realized a moment later that it was the whole Sweet Valley High cheerleading squad. There were dozens of other Sweet Valley students milling around, too, he noticed proudly. Everyone would see how fantastic Robin was.

As he leaned back against the fence and crossed his arms, his mind went back over the story Robin had choked out the night before. George's jaw tightened as he pictured her standing up to her bossy aunt.

That know-it-all never even asked Robin what she wanted to do, he said to himself indignantly. A flickering doubt passed through his mind, making him feel slightly uneasy, but he didn't know why.

A rousing cheer from the right brought him back to the present. Craning his neck, he could see a dozen girls in sleek tank suits approaching the pool to begin the warm-up session. At the back of the group came Robin, and George felt his heart lurch painfully when he saw her. She looked so alone, he thought with a surge of compassion. She was walking with her head down, and there was no spring in her step. She seemed to listen impassively as Dina Taylor gave her some last-minute coaching.

There was a general shuffling and an expectant, cheerful babble from the spectators. Everyone from Sweet Valley High knew about the rivalry between Robin and Tracy, and they were ready for an exciting showdown. A lone voice called out, "Go, Robin!" and a scattering of applause from the cheerleaders followed. George grinned to himself.

Robin's coach spoke to the girls by the diving board, then nodded firmly. Without further preparation Tracy King climbed up onto the board. She squared her shoulders and strode quickly to the end of the board. Both feet came down hard, and she sprang high into the air in a perfect, graceful jackknife. She sliced into the water to rousing applause.

"I wish I could do that," someone near George commented admiringly. "She makes it look so easy."

George felt a rush of jealousy. Wait until they see Robin—she is ten times better than Tracy, he said to himself. He watched impatiently while four other girls took their turns. Then Robin hoisted herself up the ladder.

She paused for a moment, seeming to judge the length of the board. Then she drew a deep breath and paced to the end. Turning, she put her arms out to steady herself and executed a clean back somersault in the pike position, entering the water feetfirst.

George beamed proudly but sensed that Robin could have done better. He had watched her often enough to know it wasn't a perfect dive.

Robin pulled herself, dripping, out of the water, and walked somberly to the end of the line again. It was obvious to George that she had no spirit, no confidence, no drive.

Her family is doing this to her, George told himself, gritting his teeth in anger. A quick glance through the crowd showed him that they weren't even there. Robin had mentioned her aunt's objection to diving—but not even showing up! That was too much. No wonder Robin was so depressed.

"Hi, George."

He turned and found Elizabeth Wakefield just stepping up beside him. "Hi," he said, smiling.

"How's Robin doing? I just got here."

"Well—they're still warming up," he explained. He cast a quick glance toward the diving board and felt a tug of anxiety. "She doesn't look too good so far, but she's only taken one dive," he added.

Elizabeth gave him a sympathetic smile. "Is she OK, do you think? I called her last night, and she sounded awfully depressed."

Nodding in agreement, George replied, "It's her family." He frowned across the crowded pool enclosure. "Everyone's giving her such a hassle about going to college in New York, when all she wants is to stay here."

"She does? Then why did she bother to apply?" Elizabeth mused.

George stared at her in surprise. "She only applied because they made her." He heard the doubt in his own voice, however, and he looked away in sudden confusion. Robin was just mounting the diving board again.

"Oh, there she is," Elizabeth said.

Biting his lip, George watched as Robin bounded off the end of the board and did a single tuck to a layout—an easy dive for her. Water splashed around her as she slipped into the water slightly off-center, her arms wavering. He winced.

Can she actually want to go? he asked himself desperately. *Is she really thinking about it? Is that why she's so upset?*

Instinctively he knew that was the reason, and at once he realized he was as guilty as her family was. Instead of being supportive and helping her come to one of the most important decisions of her life, he had been pouting and whining and acting like a spoiled brat. A wave of shame swept over him.

And the night before, when Robin was so upset and should have been gearing up for the competition, he had done the same thing. He was mortified to remember what he had said about Robin's mother and her aunt. After all, he was as much to blame as they were. They had tried manipulating Robin's feelings, and so had he. And she had been trying so frantically to keep all of them happy that she had made herself miserable in the process.

"But she's here anyway," he said under his breath.

Elizabeth turned to him, a puzzled expression on her face. "What?"

He shrugged. "I was just thinking—Robin's pretty special."

"I know that," Elizabeth said.

"And she deserves a lot of respect, too," he went on, turning to search for Robin in the crowd of divers. In spite of everything, she was going through with the diving championships. In spite of her aunt's unreasonable objections, in spite of his own immature tantrums, in spite of all the other pressures people had been loading onto her.

And Robin was also insisting on reaching her decision about Sarah Lawrence in her own time, too, George realized. No matter what, she wasn't letting anyone push her into something that she wasn't sure about. That was what the previous night had been about, only he had been too hung up on himself to notice it at the time.

"That aunt of hers doesn't know what she's up against," George muttered, grinning. "Robin is one person who can't be pushed around. And I'm going to show her, too."

"George Warren, I guess you must be making sense to yourself, but you sure aren't making sense to me," Elizabeth said with an airy laugh. She shook her head. "What are you talking about?"

He smiled at her. "I'm not sure yet, but give me a minute and I'll figure it out."

Robin drew a shaky breath, trying to steady her nerves. She was diving terribly, and she knew it, even without Tracy's taunting smirks. Part of the problem was that she didn't trust herself to attempt her more difficult dives. Even though they had a higher degree of difficulty and were worth more points if done well, Robin didn't feel confident enough to try them. The problem was, when the judging started, she *had* to do them whether she felt up to it or not.

Nervously she rubbed one foot over the other and bit her lower lip. Before all diving meets, the competitors had to register the dives they would perform with the judges, and when she listed her dives, she had felt a lot more confident than she did now.

Now she was committed to the hardest dives she knew. Diving competitions were divided into two sections, the springboard and the platform dives. From the springboard, each diver was responsible for five compulsory dives: one in each category of forward, backward, reverse, inward, and twisting. After that, each competitor had five voluntary dives, choosing from the same categories. Off the platform, each diver had to complete four compulsory dives and four voluntary. And with all the possible combinations of somersaults, pikes, layouts, and tucks, there were dozens of dives in each group of varying difficulty. Unfortunately, Robin and Dina had decided she would go for the most difficult ones. It was too late to change the choices now.

"You're looking a little—sloppy," Tracy whispered with a smug smile.

Robin narrowed her eyes at her neighbor and clenched her jaw. "Just warming up," she muttered, pulling irritably on the edge of her suit.

"Oh, is that what it was?"

Robin turned away, too depressed to argue or defend herself. Besides, what defense was there? There was no way she could say with a straight face that she was in top form. She was in rock-bottom form, and she didn't think it would get any better.

"Girls, be sure to take a few trial runs off the five meter," Dina said, putting a hand on each girl's shoulder and glancing at the platform. She gave Robin an encouraging smile. "Now come on. Just loosen up and forget about the crowd."

A choking feeling in her throat kept Robin from answering. She just nodded and looked away. Across the pool she could make out the faces of many of her friends. With a wistful smile she spotted Annie, who had come to the competition in spite of everything. *What a jerk I was,* Robin realized sadly. *She probably hates me now.*

Her eyes traveled through the crowd again, seeking George. Finally she caught sight of him talking to Elizabeth with a concentrated look on his face. She wished he would look up and smile at her, but he didn't seem to be paying much attention. Sighing, she dropped her eyes to the ground again.

"Attention, please! There will be a slight delay before competition begins. Judging will commence in one half hour!" the announcer blared out suddenly.

Robin looked blankly at Dina. "What's the problem? Why are we waiting?"

"I don't know," her coach replied, frowning with concern. "I'll go find out."

As Dina hurried away, Robin felt her agitation shift into high gear. She began shifting nervously from foot to foot, hugging her arms across her chest to keep warm. Delays always made things worse. Muscles had time to cramp up, doubts increased. Anything could happen.

"Come on, come on," she muttered under her breath. "I just want to get this *over* with!"

She glanced up across the crowd, looking for George again. But even as she spotted him, he suddenly wheeled away from Elizabeth and began shouldering his way through the crowd to the exit. Robin's stomach turned over.

He's too bored even to stay and watch, she realized miserably. *He doesn't care.*

And then as she closed her eyes in exhaustion, she added to herself, *Maybe I should just give up. What's the point in going through with it anyway?*

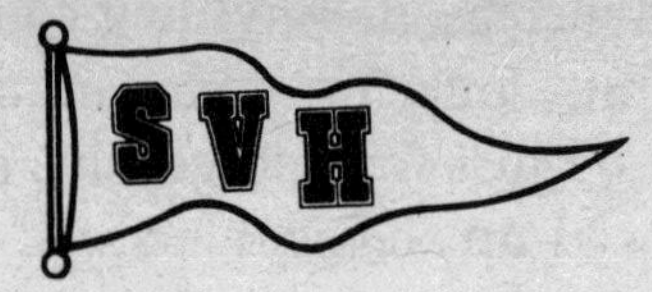

Thirteen

Shivering, Robin paced back and forth. Her thin nylon tank suit was drying quickly, but she felt cold in spite of the sun. Cold and alone.

"It's been at least half an hour," another diver, Karen Doyle, complained edgily. "I don't get what the big problem is."

"I don't know. It was something about one of the judges—he isn't here yet. I guess they're waiting for him to show up," someone else speculated.

I can't do this, Robin told herself.

Over near the judges' stand she could see Dina talking urgently with one of the officials. Robin knew that if she backed out of the competition, Dina would be furious and disappointed. Her coach had put in hours and hours of time to get Robin ready for this competition, and Dina was the one person Robin refused to disappoint.

But if this competition doesn't get started in five minutes, I just don't think I can go through with it. She was too nervous, too depressed, too everything.

A few yards away Tracy was busily stretching her muscles, keeping them limber and warm during the wait. Backing out meant Tracy would win for sure, Robin realized. But winning just didn't seem important anymore.

"Robin," Dina said, coming up behind her with a warm, coaxing smile, "hang in there. I think we're going to get going pretty soon."

Robin stared at her coach and swallowed hard. There was a huge lump in her throat. "Dina, I don't—"

"Ladies and gentlemen," called the announcer.

Dina jumped and gripped Robin's arm excitedly. "There!"

Stifling her words, Robin bowed her head as the announcer continued.

"Ladies and gentlemen, our apologies for the delay. We are now ready to begin with the springboard diving segment of our competition. Our apologies to the divers, too."

Robin felt a warm pressure on her arm. "Go for it," Dina whispered with a reassuring squeeze.

"And remember, watch your layouts, Robin. I want that body *straight* from head to toe."

Robin nodded dully and climbed onto the diving board.

"Robin Wilson's first compulsory dive is a forward somersault in the pike position."

Robin nodded toward the judges and straightened her back. She just had to do the best she could. Dina's advice came back to her as she ran to the end of the board and pushed off and up. Lifting her hips, she tucked her head and swung her legs up and around, keeping her knees rigid. She stretched out, but off the vertical and with her arms wobbling. As she entered the pool feetfirst and the water closed over her head, she knew it was far from a perfect dive.

Shaking her head, she kicked up toward the surface and waited for her scores to be announced. Of the five, the highest and the lowest would be cancelled out, and the remaining three added . . . then multiplied by the degree-of-difficulty factor.

"Seven-point-five, seven-point-five, eight-point-two-five, eight-point-zero, seven-point-five," came the announcement when she had finished her dives.

As Robin heaved herself up out of the water, she gave the crowd one more scanning glance. Then she stiffened in surprise. George was back, edging hurriedly through the crowd. And behind him were her aunt, her mother, and Troy and Adam!

Stunned, Robin took a step toward the edge of the pool, and her hands rose unconsciously to her mouth. She felt her heart race with hope, anxiety, and confusion. How had George gotten them to come? And what did it mean that they *had* come?

As she watched her family climbing into the bleachers, George turned and met her eyes across the water. With a big smile, he gave her a thumbs-up sign. Robin's heart pounded even harder. She stood in total bewilderment while the next four competitors took their first compulsory dives. It was only when Tracy scored three nines that Robin shook the fog out of her head. She glanced at George again, a trembling, uncertain smile on her lips.

"Robin, you're up. Let's go for it," Dina urged, just behind her.

Reluctantly Robin pulled herself away from George's loving gaze and walked slowly toward the diving board. She placed her hands firmly on the cool metal ladder and put her foot on the first step.

With each of the three short steps she felt lighter and stronger. Each rung took her one bit farther from the misery and gloom she had been buried in. At the top she paused and then looked at the crowd across the sparkling water.

"Go, Robin!" yelled Maria Santelli, waving her arms above her head. The other cheerleaders all shouted and applauded, and Robin felt a surge of excitement and gratitude. Then Robin's gaze met Annie's, and Robin lifted her hand in a little wave. A huge smile broke over Annie's face.

Robin turned her head to look at George again, and she felt a strong bond of love and support reaching up and across the water from him. From her perch, it seemed she was seeing things from a whole new perspective.

"I can do this," she whispered to herself. "I *will*."

"Robin Wilson has chosen a back somersault, layout, for her second compulsory dive," came the announcement over the P.A. system.

With increasing confidence Robin positioned herself on the end of the board, facing the ladder. Then she swung her arms up and arched backward, her body one smooth, graceful line. The dive looked simple, but as Dina had explained to Robin over and over, the layout was one of the hardest positions to execute perfectly. As Robin's toes sliced into the water, she knew she *had* done it perfectly.

Yes! she told herself as she shot up through the water. *I'm back!*

The crowd of spectators was applauding as she surfaced, and Robin grinned broadly through the water that streamed down her face. She swam quickly to the ladder at the side of the pool and pulled herself up. Still halfway in the water, she waited for her scores to be announced.

"Nine-point-five, nine-point-five, nine-point-zero, nine-point-zero, nine-point-five," the announcer's voice crackled through the speakers.

Dina leaned down to Robin with an earnest smile. "Good girl. Keep it steady, now. You're doing great. The twists and doubles are going to pull your total ahead, too."

Nodding, Robin climbed up onto the pavement and stood with her arms folded. She watched the others take their turns. Tracy was pulling in near-perfect scores, and Robin knew the race was on.

With six divers altogether, it took quite a while to get through the springboard segment of the competition. But Robin knew every single dive mattered. Her concentration didn't waver for an instant, regardless of the noise of the crowd, the decisions of the judges, or the speculative looks Tracy kept sending her. Because her scores and Tracy's were multiplied by higher degree-of-difficulty factors, the two of them began climbing ahead of the others in total points. It was becoming a contest between just two players.

Finally it was time to move up to the platform. The order of the divers was changed, and Tracy went first, casting a challenging smile at Robin as she mounted the ladder. She bounded to the end of the board and jumped into a soaring swan dive. Her back was arched perfectly, her arms held at precisely the right angle. At the last minute she tucked into a front flip and sliced vertically into the pool with virtually no splash at all.

Another loud burst of applause broke out, and Robin felt grudging admiration. Tracy's form was excellent. Everything that went into a perfect dive was there: skill, grace, strength, and beauty. Tracy deserved the applause.

The announcer gave Tracy's scores: "Nine-point-seven, nine-point-five, nine-point-seven, nine-point-five, and nine-point-two-five."

"You've got a lot of work to do if you want to get ahead," Tracy said with a grin as she climbed out of the water. She met Robin's eyes challengingly. "Think you can make it, Robin?"

Robin raised her chin defiantly. "Just watch, Tracy. I'll show you."

And I will show you, *too,* she added silently, looking up at her aunt in the bleachers. She remembered what her aunt had said about talent: it wasn't enough on its own; success took hard work and dedication, too. Well, Robin was going to show her aunt Fiona that she had talent, too. *And* hard work and dedication. And even if diving didn't make Robin a fortune, it was just as valuable!

Her head high, she strode to the ladder and began the long climb. An expectant hush fell over the crowd as she paused at the top and narrowed her eyes at the end of the board. Her first dive had an arm stand takeoff, which she had always felt was one of her best. Because Robin did handstands so often for cheerleading, they came almost as easily as running!

She paced steadily to the end and leaned over, planting her palms on the scratchy surface of the board. Then, with enormous control, she slowly pressed up in a pike, raising her legs straight up to the sky. From that position she dropped forward and tucked her knees up to do a double somersault with a full twist. Her fingertips cut cleanly into the water, and her body followed in a straight plunge toward the blue-painted bottom.

Robin smiled underwater and kicked hard toward the surface. *Beat that, Tracy,* she thought as she broke through. Tracy met her gaze as she climbed out of the water, and Robin couldn't resist a smirk.

"Nine-point-eight, nine-point-nine, nine-point-eight, nine-point-zero, nine-point-five," came the score a few seconds later.

Robin let her breath out in a gasp of relief and pressed one hand over her pounding heart. "I'm going for it, Dina," she whispered as her coach patted her on the back.

"I know it, Robin. You're doing great."

Soon it was clear to everyone in the stands that the competition was really just between Robin and Tracy. The other divers were passable, but their scores never approached the nine-point-fives and nine-point-nines that Robin and Tracy were racking up so consistently. With each dive the tension grew thicker, until it was almost tangible.

"The contestants each have two voluntary dives remaining," the announcer reminded them. "Two dives each."

Robin hugged her arms across her chest and sat down on a bench next to Dina. "What's my score?"

Glancing at the clipboard in her hand, Dina frowned. "You're still behind Tracy."

Robin looked down at the scores her coach had been recording and gritted her teeth. Her last two dives were hard enough to put her in the lead if she scored nine-fives or better.

"Tracy's up now," Dina observed.

Robin nodded, watching her rival climbing up to the platform. Holding her breath, she kept her eyes riveted on Tracy, who pushed off backward and did an inward double flip with a half twist in a layout position. Robin let her breath out in a small gasp and bit her lip in consternation. Was it her imagination, or had Tracy's legs wobbled apart there at the end?

The scores were announced after a brief delay. "Nine-point-zero, nine-point-zero, eight-point-five, eight-point-zero, nine-point-zero."

Tracy's jaw was tightly clenched as she passed Robin and sat down, and Robin felt a surge of hope. She could do it. With a bit of luck and a lot of concentration, she could do it.

As she crossed to the ladder, she stole a quick look across to the waiting crowd. George and her family were all leaning forward eagerly—even her aunt. Each time she stepped up to the rung of the ladder they inched forward a little more. They were *with* her, she realized gratefully. She raised her face to the top of the ladder and climbed the last three rungs. Then she began readying herself mentally for a reverse two-and-a-half somersault, full twist.

Robin's eyes darted to the ground again, searching for Dina. Her coach nodded and mouthed, "Go for it."

With a surge of adrenaline jetting through

her veins, Robin sprang to the end of the board and reached up. Kick, over, over, twist—*straight*—yes! It was over in a matter of seconds, and Robin was shooting up through the water again, smiling with anticipation. The dive had been perfect. She could feel it.

"Nine-point-five, nine-point-five, ten, nine-point-nine, ten," came the scores.

A roar of excitement erupted from the crowd, and Robin gasped with relief. Her cheeks hurt from smiling so much, but she reminded herself that there was still one dive to go. She hurried to Dina to check the point totals. Tracy was still ahead by a few points, but Robin had taken up some of the slack. She waited impatiently for the other divers to complete their turns.

She was so nervous now, she thought she might be sick. But it was a good kind of nervousness, a fluttery, adrenaline-charged anticipation that kept forcing a smile to her lips—not the miserable dread she had been living with for the past two weeks. Pressing her elbows into her sides to keep from shaking, Robin watched Tracy climb for her last dive. Next to her, Dina was sitting tight-jawed, clutching the clipboard with white-knuckled hands.

As Tracy ran to the end of the board, Robin could sense her timing was off. And as her rival tucked into the first of two front rolls, Robin knew Tracy's winning streak was over. For now, at least. She tried not to smile, but she couldn't help it. After the high and low scores were cancelled, Tracy had two nines, and an eight-point-seven-five.

Dina was rapidly punching numbers into a calculator, but Robin did the arithmetic in her head. The difficulty factor on Robin's last dive was a two-five, only half a point from the highest degree. So if Robin scored three tens, multiplying thirty by two-point-five, she'd have another seventy-five points. That would put her two points ahead of Tracy, in first place.

"Go for the perfect dive, Robin," Dina whispered, echoing her thoughts. She looked Robin in the eye, a faint smile on her lips. "You can do it."

Robin stood up and adjusted a shoulder strap. She couldn't even look at the crowd in case it threw off her concentration. Everything was riding on the last critical dive.

"This is Robin Wilson's last voluntary dive," the announcer informed the crowd. "A flying forward two-and-a-half somersault pike, half-twist."

A whoop of enthusiasm rippled through the crowd. Mingled shouts of "Go, Robin!" and "Go for it!" accompanied her up the ladder.

She swallowed hard and braved a lightning-quick glance into the bleachers. Her aunt was on the edge of her seat, her hands clasped fervently in front of her. Their eyes met, and Robin managed a quavering smile. Fiona Maxwell nodded in encouragement.

Then Robin squared her shoulders and drew a deep breath. She gripped the surface of the platform with her toes, feeling the rough texture that would give her the traction she needed to build up speed. She bounced lightly once on her heels and pushed off toward the end of the board.

In the air, everything happened too fast to think through consciously. Robin let her body roll and roll and straighten and twist, and then the shock of cold water slipped up around her, and she plunged down in a wild swirl of bubbles. She arched up and kicked toward the surface.

Surging up, she shook the water out of her face and turned quickly toward the judges' stand. She treaded water, breathing hard while they deliberated. Then the announcer tapped the microphone.

"Ten—"

Wild applause broke out.

"Nine-point-five—"

The cheerleaders let loose a cry.

"Ten, Ten, Ten! A perfect score for Robin Wilson!"

Robin threw herself backward in the water, letting herself submerge for a breathless, ecstatic moment. Victory! She had done it!

As she swam to the ladder, she could see George and her family running toward her around the edge of the pool. She had won—more than just first place, too. She had definitely *won*! With a feeling of inner control that she hadn't had in weeks, Robin hauled herself out of the water to face George and her family. Now she knew what to say.

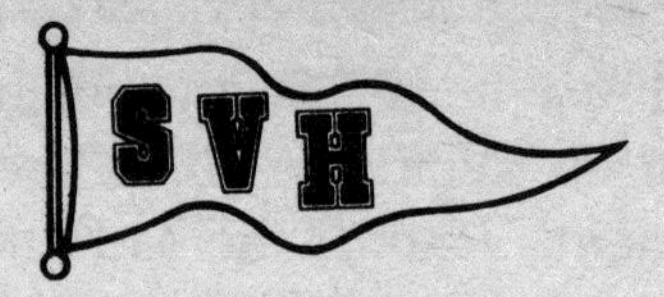

Fourteen

"Oh, Robin! I'm so proud of you," Mrs. Wilson cried, swooping down to kiss Robin's cheek. She took both her hands. "That was just wonderful."

"Yeah," Troy put in. "Awesome, Robin."

George put one arm across her shoulders and kissed her swiftly on the lips. But Robin was looking at her aunt.

There was a long, appraising moment between them as their eyes met. Finally a smile broke over Fiona Maxwell's face.

"I must say, Robin. I'm impressed. Very impressed."

Robin's heart swelled with pride, and she opened her mouth to speak. But before she could say anything, Dina hurried to her side.

"Robin! I think this could do it—this could definitely clinch an athletic scholarship for you. And believe me, I'll be pushing for you every step," she added with a beaming smile.

Robin stared at her coach in disbelief. An athletic scholarship? That could solve everything! Now her decision was even firmer. She faced her aunt.

"I'm sorry about what I said last night, Aunt Fiona. Believe me, I appreciate it very much that you were willing to pay for Sarah Lawrence. But I'm not ready to go to college yet. I'm going to stay at Sweet Valley High for my senior year and then decide."

Fiona Maxwell met her eyes evenly, without a word.

"Partly it's because of my diving," Robin went on, frowning thoughtfully as she puzzled through her tumbling feelings. "Diving is very important to me, but making my own decisions is even more important. At least for now, I want to stay in California."

From the corner of her eye, Robin caught a slightly smug look on George's face. She rounded on him swiftly. "And not because *you* want me to," she said. He looked abashed as she went on. "It's because *I* want to. I want to decide *where* and *when* I go to school."

"But, Robin," Mrs. Wilson said, her voice

sounding nervous. "Robin, how are you going to pay for it? I mean, a scholarship is fine, but that won't—"

"I can get a student loan. I can get a part-time job. There are plenty of ways to get through college if you're willing to work hard enough."

Robin's aunt sniffed loudly and arched her eyebrows. "Diving, part-time job, college. If you do all three, you won't do any of them well," she commented cynically.

"I'm going to try," Robin insisted. She lifted her chin defiantly. "And I will do it."

"Oh, Robin!" Fiona Maxwell said. "You're just as stubborn as I am, I can see that. What I'm trying to say is that I'll be glad to help wherever you decide to go to school—no strings attached," she added gruffly.

For a moment Robin just stared at her aunt in shock. She couldn't believe what she was hearing! Then she laughed and jumped forward to envelop her aunt in a tight hug. But she pulled back the next instant, realizing she was still soaking wet.

There was a tense pause while everyone looked at Fiona Maxwell. Her expensive silk suit was dark with water marks. She stared down at her front for a second, then raised her eyes to Robin.

"Oh, I'm sorry," Robin said, her eyes wide.

But her aunt smiled wryly. "Don't worry. I can afford it."

Behind Robin, George let out a whoop of laughter, which he quickly stifled. But Robin felt a giggle rise in her own throat. "Well, I—" She broke off, trying not to laugh.

Fiona Maxwell shrugged. "Of course I'd still be overjoyed if you decide to go to Sarah Lawrence next year, but I won't force you. I won't try to control you—I can see it would be a losing battle."

"I guess that's true," Robin's mother said, eyeing her with admiration. "Well, anyway, it looks like your friends want to congratulate you, sweetie. We'll go home and get a celebration picnic going, how's that?"

Robin nodded, her eyes still on her aunt. "That's great. Just great."

George put his arm around her again as her family left. When they were gone, Robin looked at George with a question in her eyes.

"When I realized what we were all doing to you, I had to get them to come," he explained, smiling at her with love and pride. "I had to make them see how unfair they were being and that it was so petty not to watch you compete. It took a lot of talking, too," he added.

Robin touched his cheek, too moved to speak. It meant more than anything else to her that

George finally understood what she had been going through.

"But what really clinched it was when I told your aunt you were up against Tracy King. She nearly had a fit," he continued, his voice filled with laughter. "I remembered what you told me about her hating that dumb statue in their front yard. I figured it would work."

"I guess it did." Robin giggled, suddenly light-hearted and giddy with success. She turned as she glimpsed a crowd of her friends from the corner of her eye. For a few noisy, bustling minutes, cheerleaders and friends from Sweet Valley milled around, clapping her on the back and hugging her.

Then, over the shoulder of Elizabeth Wakefield, who was hugging her for the third time, Robin saw Annie hanging back at the end of the group. Their eyes met, and Robin smiled ruefully. Breaking away, Robin walked over to her friend.

"Annie—I'm really sorry I acted like such an idiot," she murmured, searching her friend's face for signs of forgiveness. "Can you stand to talk to me again?"

Annie's mouth twisted into a little half smile, and her green eyes twinkled. "Mmm . . . I *guess* so."

"Oh, great!" Robin exclaimed, throwing her

arms around Annie. "I'm really glad, Annie. I really am."

Annie nodded, tears shining in her eyes. "Me, too."

A few feet away, Elizabeth and Jessica watched the reunion with mixed reactions. Jessica was rolling her eyes in disgust at the emotional display, but Elizabeth was smiling happily.

"Boy, am I glad that worked out," Elizabeth said. "I thought I had definitely screwed things up."

Jessica tossed her head. "Oh, big deal."

"Jess!" Elizabeth exclaimed. "Sometimes I think you're *totally* insensitive."

"Not totally," Jessica corrected. Her eyes twinkled as she looked back at her twin. "Anyway, let's go home, all right? I've got a date tonight, and I need to work on my tan this afternoon."

They turned and headed across the lawn toward the parking lot. Elizabeth stole a quick glance at her sister. Obviously Jessica had gotten over Alex Kane without any problems. As Elizabeth's thoughts turned back to her sister's escapade with the elusive music student, she remembered the recorder. *Her* recorder now.

"You're sure you don't mind about me taking the recorder?" she asked anxiously.

Jessica shrugged and opened the car door.

"Nah. I really think it's the dullest thing on earth, to tell you the truth."

"Good." Elizabeth climbed into the Fiat next to her sister. "I think I'll call Julie Porter, then, and see if she can help me out with it. She plays the flute, the piano, *and* the recorder."

Jessica started the car and craned her neck to back out. "Be my guest, Liz."

Elizabeth laughed. "Thanks, Jess. I think I will."

Later that afternoon, after dropping Jessica off at Lila Fowler's house, Elizabeth headed for the quiet eucalyptus-lined street Julie Porter lived on. She hummed cheerfully along with the radio, her thoughts racing ahead. Julie had been surprised but glad when Elizabeth called her and asked if they could get together. Over the past few years they had drifted apart somewhat, although Elizabeth still liked Julie very much. It was just because Julie spent so much time practicing and studying and taking master classes in piano that their schedules didn't come together very often.

But that could be changing now, Elizabeth decided. She was smiling with anticipation as she pulled up in front of the Porters' house. As she stepped out of the Fiat, the front door opened and Julie and a tall, dark-haired boy came out.

She recognized him as Julie's next door neighbor and a junior at Sweet Valley High.

"Hi!" Elizabeth called out, waving. She swung her bag over her shoulder and jogged up to the porch.

"Hi, Liz. You know Josh Bowen, don't you?" the petite redhead said.

Liz had seen Josh in the hallways, but she had never been in a class with him.

Josh smiled shyly and dug his hands into his pockets. "Hi. I've read your articles—I've seen you around school, too," he confessed. "But you probably wouldn't remember me."

"Of course I remember you," Elizabeth retorted with an easy laugh. "You just haven't turned up in my 'Eyes and Ears' column—yet." She turned twinkling eyes to Julie and wondered briefly if there was anything romantic between the two.

But Julie didn't have that certain sparkle when she looked at Josh, it seemed. Apparently they were just friends. "See you later, Josh," Julie said.

"OK—bye. Nice to see you, Liz." Josh trotted down the steps and headed for his house.

"Sooo . . ." Turning to her friend, Elizabeth raised her eyebrows in a questioning look. "He seems nice."

"Josh? Sure, he's a good guy," her friend

replied, leading the way inside. "We hang out together a lot. Come on in."

The Porters' house was one that was completely devoted to music, and it was evident wherever Elizabeth looked. Dr. Porter, Julie's widowed father, played first violin for the Los Angeles Symphony and also taught music. Julie's life revolved around piano and flute and music theory. The only one who wasn't musical was her sister, Johanna. The living room was dominated by a concert grand piano. Shelves of records, compact discs, and musical scores lined the room.

"I got out some of my old flute music," Julie was saying, her brown eyes dark and serious with a true music-lover's dedication. "I think it'll be fine for recorder, too. I don't know how advanced you are."

"Not at all!" Elizabeth said with a rueful smile. She set her bag down by the piano and looked anxiously at the sheet music. "I've really just started."

Julie grinned. "No problem. We can work on some duets for beginners."

"You're going to think I'm really terrible." Feeling self-conscious, she took out the recorder. But she didn't want to waste Julie's time by making a lot of apologetic comments, so she just squared her shoulders and took a deep breath. "OK, maestro," she quipped. "Let's go."

After an hour Elizabeth was beginning to feel dizzy, and she waved her hand for a halt. "Mind if we take a break?" she begged.

Julie made a minor adjustment to her recorder and blew a rippling string of notes before she shook her head with a smile. "No problem. You're doing great. You know . . ." she went on, suddenly reddening slightly. She lowered her eyes and said somewhat awkwardly, "I wanted to ask you if you know anything about the fraternities at school."

Curious, Elizabeth cocked her head to one side. She didn't know what made Julie bring up the subject, but she didn't want to be nosy about it. "Well, a little bit. Why?"

Julie blushed unexpectedly. "It's just that, well, Josh wants to pledge Phi Epsilon, that's all. So he's been hanging around lately with some of those guys—like—like Bruce Patman, for instance."

"Oh," Elizabeth said, nodding in perplexity. She didn't know where the conversation was leading. Maybe Julie wanted to know what kind of guys Josh was getting in with. But if Julie was looking for a good character reference for Bruce Patman, she had come to the wrong place! Although Bruce had had a brief change of character earlier in the year when he had started dating Regina Morrow, he quickly went back to his old ways after her tragic death. Elizabeth wasn't exactly a fan of his, and she knew that Julie's friend could do a lot better than hanging around with stuck-up, selfish Bruce. Smiling uncertainly, she waited for Julie to go on.

"Didn't Jessica used to go out with him? Bruce, I mean?"

Elizabeth laughed. "Well, it was a pretty short romance, believe me! Jessica doesn't like *anyone* to outshine her, and Bruce was always trying to do that!"

"I guess he does have a lot of self-confidence," Julie agreed. She kept fiddling with the mouthpiece of her recorder, not meeting Elizabeth's eyes.

In Elizabeth's opinion *self-confidence* was not the word for what Bruce Patman had. A mile-wide ego was more like it. She was about to point out the difference, but something about Julie's attitude struck her as odd. She frowned, confused.

"Why the sudden interest in Bruce Patman?" she asked, deciding to be direct.

To her surprise Julie blushed even redder, her freckles almost disappearing in the pink. "No reason," Julie said, standing up quickly and taking some more music from a shelf. "Just curious."

Could it be possible, Elizabeth wondered, that serious, dedicated Julie Porter was interested in Bruce Patman? He was just about the most egotistical, self-centered boy in the senior class! For someone as sweet and unpretentious as Julie to like him seemed almost impossible.

But as Elizabeth stared at Julie's blushing profile, she had the nagging suspicion that that was exactly what was going on!

***Does Julie Porter have her sights set on Bruce Patman? Find out in Sweet Valley High #47,* TROUBLEMAKER.**